BOOKS BY DAVID WALLIAMS:

The Boy in the Dress
Mr Stink
Billionaire Boy
Gangsta Granny
Ratburger
Demon Dentist
Awful Auntie
Grandpa's Great Escape
The Midnight Gang
Bad Dad
The Ice Monster
The Beast of Buckingham Palace

Fing
Slime

The World's Worst Children
The World's Worst Children 2
The World's Worst Children 3
The World's Worst Teachers

ALSO AVAILABLE IN PICTURE BOOK:

The Slightly Annoying Elephant
The First Hippo on the Moon
The Bear Who Went Boo!
The Queen's Orang-utan
There's a Snake in My School!
Boogie Bear
Geronimo
The Creature Choir

David Walliams

THE WORLD'S WORST

PARENTS

Illustrated in glorious colour by

Tony Ross

HarperCollins *Children's Books*

DAVID WALLIAMS

TONY ROSS

For Albert and Eddie,
Much love,
David x

Dedicated to the
World's Best Parents,
MINE!
T.R.

First published in Great Britain by HarperCollins *Children's Books* in 2020
HarperCollins *Children's Books* is a division of HarperCollins*Publishers* Ltd,
HarperCollins Publishers, 1 London Bridge Street, London SE1 9GF
The HarperCollins website address is www.harpercollins.co.uk

10 9 8 7 6 5 4 3 2 1

Text copyright © David Walliams 2020
Illustrations copyright © Tony Ross 2020
Cover lettering of author's name copyright © Quentin Blake 2010
All rights reserved.
HB ISBN 978–0–00–830579–6   TPB ISBN 978–0–00–843030–6

David Walliams and Tony Ross assert the moral right to be identified as the
author and illustrator of the work respectively.
Printed and bound in the UK by CPI Colour Ltd.

Find out more about HarperCollins and the environment at
www.harpercollins.co.uk/green

THANK-YOUS

I would like to thank...

Tony Ross, *my illustrator.* Tony's dad was a conjurer and put him onstage to do some easy tricks, without telling him how to do them. That was quite embarrassing for a seven-year-old.

Executive Publisher **Ann-Janine Murtagh.** Ann-Janine's dad loved dancing and used to say he had "the music in his feet"! He would twirl her around until she was giddy, which was great fun when she was six, but really embarrassing when she was sixteen!

HarperCollins CEO, **Charlie Redmayne.** Charlie's dad assumed that speaking English loudly in a French accent would be an effective means of communicating when in France!

My literary agent, **Paul Stevens.** Paul's mother made him dance with her at her birthday party whilst she was dressed as Scarlett O'Hara from *Gone with the Wind.* He says, "I'm glad. I love to dance now."

My editor, **Harriet Wilson.** Her mum sewed all Harriet's clothes herself because she said homemade was better than shop bought. It wasn't.

Art editor **Kate Burns.** To celebrate the Silver Jubilee, Kate's parents made her dress up as a Spanish flamenco dancer and ride through the village on a painted float made out of a pig hut – in the rain.

Publishing Manager **Samantha Stewart.** Sam's strict bedtime was 6pm even when she was a teenager! (That's why she read so many books by torchlight...)

Creative Director **Val Brathwaite.** Val's mum was keen to encourage her kids to love opera and so played it full blast when they got home from school. This was particularly embarrassing when Val's friends came round for tea.

Designer **Kate Clarke.** Kate remembers her dad singing "The One and Only" by Chesney Hawkes on a loop for weeks on end, as he'd decided it was his favourite song of all time. It drove her and her brother nuts!

Designer **Elorine Grant.** Elorine's mum made her eat porridge and now even the smell of it makes her sick...

Designer **Matthew Kelly.** Matt's mum picked him up from school in a pink Morris Minor that was so rusty you could see the road through the floor!

Designer **Sally Griffin.** Sally was sitting in the garden with her very first boyfriend, and her mum and sister decided to throw frozen peas at them from a bedroom window!

My audio editor, **Tanya Hougham.** When Tanya was little, she was a tomboy, but her mum insisted on dressing her up in the biggest, itchiest, frilliest dresses... THE WORST!

Head of Marketing **Alex Cowan.** Alex's mum put his favourite roll-neck on a boil wash and shrank it to doll-size.

My PR Director, **Geraldine Stroud.** Geraldine's mum used to cut her fringe with the craft scissors to save on visits to hairdressers! It never ended well...

David Walliams

A letter from
David Walliams' mum

Dear Children of the World,

Hmm. Well. Yes. Mmm. What do I think about this latest offering, ***The World's Worst Parents***? I must say my son is really taking liberties this time. I have looked after him for most of my adult life. I still wash his dirty underpants to this day! Let me tell you, children, they are not a pretty sight. Oh no. Not pretty at all. Like an abstract painting. In smellovision.

Then my David has the nerve to write a book about awful mothers and fathers! May I suggest he writes a book entitled ***The World's Worst Sons***? Then he could put himself in there!

In fact, there are so many dreadful things he has said and done that it could stretch to a hundred volumes.

Or, better still, how about my David writes **_The World's Worst David Walliams Books_**? I am not sure there will be enough room to fit all of them in there. That is because my David has written **937** books! **937!** And that is just this morning. All 937 of them deserve a place, especially this latest offering. I urge you NOT to read it. Please STOP reading this right now!

Thank you.

Oh, you still are? That is annoying. Well, I did warn you, but you didn't listen! This book is the **_worst of the worst._ Worsterest.** Which is not even a word. Stick that in your **Walliamsictionary**!

The worst thing of all is that it is not even me, David's mother, writing this introduction. He is writing it pretending to be me! That is the kind of son he is. Despicable.

Yours not even,

*Mrs Kathleen Walliams**

* This isn't even my name. My name is Kathleen Williams, but my **idiot** son changed his name to something stupid.

CONTENTS

PETER PONG

THERE ARE **HUNDREDS** of ways in which parents can embarrass their children:

Spitting on a handkerchief and wiping your chin with it.

"SPUT! HOLD STILL!"

"YUCK! GET OFF ME!"

Wheeling you around in a pram even though you grew out of it years ago.

"OOH! MY *beautiful* IKKLE BABY!"

"I'M NOT A BABY! I AM THIRTEEN YEARS OLD!"

Making you put on a song-and-dance show every time your grandmother comes to visit.

"DANCE! DANCE! DANCE FOR US!"

"I AM NOT A PERFORMING MONKEY!"

"DANCE, MONKEY, DANCE!"

Giving you a big slobbery kiss at the school gates.

"MWAH!"

"GET OFF ME! I AM COVERED IN SLOBBER!"

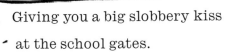

THE WORLD'S WORST PARENTS

Dressing you up like a Victorian sailor boy for a family wedding.

"YOU LOOK delightful!"

"I LOOK LIKE I SHOULD HAVE GONE DOWN WITH THE SHIP!"

Telling you over and over again that it was so much harder in **their** day.

"We didn't have any sweets in my day, my lad. If we were hungry, we would have to suck on a pebble."

"OH, GIVE IT A REST, DAD! YOUR MUM IS THE QUEEN!"

Cutting your fringe with a pair of nail scissors.

"HOLD STILL!"

"MUM! IT'S ALL WONKY!"

"WONKY IS COOL! ALL THE KIDS ARE DOING IT!"

"NO, IT ISN'T COOL AND IT NEVER WILL BE!"

Telling all your friends at your twelfth birthday party stories about exactly what you used to deposit in your nappy when you were a baby.

"When I picked her up out of her cot, I thought it was only a number one, but by the smug look on her face I knew it had to be a number two..."

"MUM!"

However, very few parents can embarrass their child as much as this man.

Peter and his wife, Penny, had a daughter, and they named her Ping. Ping Pong.

That wasn't the embarrassing thing. The thing that was embarrassing was Peter Pong's feet. The man had the cheesiest feet in the world.*

* WALLYFACT: For many years, the world-record holder for stinkiest feet was a little girl – Rita Reek. Rita could empty her school in seconds when she waltzed in wearing her flip-flops. The teachers and pupils who couldn't scramble out of the doors in time were knocked out cold by the stink. That meant no schoolwork for Rita! Hurrah!

Peter may have been a short man, but he was a giant in the world of **whiffs.**

If you had incredibly **cheesy** feet, it's most likely you would hide them away – put on some thick socks, and contain them in some sturdy shoes or, better still, boots.

Not Peter Pong, oh no. Peter was proud of his pong. He knew he had **stinktastic*** feet and wanted to share them with the world.

So, whatever the weather, Peter Pong would be sporting sandals. Even in deep snow! They were open-toed leather sandals so that everybody could see his corns, blisters and grotty toenails – and, of course, enjoy the **stink,** especially little people who were closest to the ground.

Short people.

What was this smell, exactly?

Cheese.

Not a nice mild Cheddar or a Wensleydale.

Oh no.

A really **stinkerocious**** runny cheese... that had been left out in the sun to curdle – for a decade.

* **Walliamsictionary:** gives the definition of "**stinktastic**" as "very, very, very, very, very, very, very, very, very, very, very, smelly".

** **Walliamsictionary:** gives the definition of "**stinkerocious**" as "very, very smelly".

The stink from Peter Pong was so strong it was actually visible. A yellowy greeny browny **gas** hummed from his feet.

HUMMM!

To cover up the smell, Peter's daughter, Ping, took up cooking. The aromas of yummy ingredients floated across the kitchen and danced around their little flat. They almost... ALMOST... cancelled out the smell of her father's feet.

Over the weeks, months and years Ping became a master chef. Every night she made something delicious for the family: pies, stews, curries, trifles, crumbles. Ping dreamed that one day she could escape the stinky family flat and become a world-famous chef with bestselling cookery books and restaurants all over the world.

So great a chef did Ping become that her mother, Penny, suggested she enter a TV cooking competition named

Cook Off. It was a very popular series where amateur chefs competed to be crowned *Cook of Cooks*. Instant fame and riches beckoned for the winner of the show as it was watched by millions of people.

Cook Off was filmed in a giant pink marquee. The competition was for grown-ups, but Ping was so gifted that she was allowed to take part even though she was only twelve.

The little girl forbade her father to come to the show. She knew those stinky feet of his could ruin it for her, **BIG TIME.** So, **stinky-feet** free, Ping made it all the way to the final, and being so talented and so young she became the hot favourite with the public to win.

The host of **Cook Off** was Tony Truffle, a big, jolly man who looked like he enjoyed his food. Truffle was famous for his outrageously obvious brown wig, brightly coloured glasses and flowery shirts. They served as a substitute for a personality, something that he lacked.

Cook Off had two judges. The first was Boby Bollywood, the owner of a famous Indian restaurant called the Taj

Mahal 2. Boby thought he was way cooler than he actually was. The second was an elderly lady and expert cook, Dame Penelope Plum. She was so *posh* she made *the Queen* look common.

Every week, the two judges would taste the dishes and give their verdict on them.

After some deliberation towards the end of the show, the *Cook of Cooks* would finally be crowned.

For the final, it was decided that the remaining competitors should prepare an **Italian** dish. Aside from Ping, there were two other amateur cooks who'd made it to the last show.

Henry Heft had made a huge impression on the viewers. He was a tattooed giant of a man who wore a beaten-up black leather biker jacket with a skull and crossbones painted on the back. Heft had impressed the judges with his *cream puffs.*

The other finalist was a **sour-faced** woman who never cracked a smile, or even uttered a word, named Vivienne Vinegar. She wore grey roll-neck jumpers and long skirts, and seemingly cut her own hair with a pair of scissors and a pudding bowl. Vivienne had wowed the judges with her **boiled eggs.**

So, the morning of the final came. Ping dashed around the supermarket with her parents to buy all the ingredients she needed to make her creamy mushroom pasta. However, when she called out for her father to reach for a block of *Italian Parmesan cheese* from the top shelf, the man was momentarily distracted by his own stinky feet. When he leaped up to reach the shelf, he released some **"under stink"**. **"Under stink"** is the worst of all the stinks as it comes from the bottom of the foot. The stench snaked all the way up from his toes to his nose, and even he was taken by surprise by the PONGTASMAGORIA.*

* Another word you will find in your *Walliamsictionary,* which includes well over a trillion made-up words.

As his wife and child gagged, the stink actually
blinded Peter for a moment. Tears welled in his eyes
at the smell and he picked up a pat of cooking fat by
mistake. This was **not** noticed until much, much later.

Once they had bought all the ingredients, the Pong
family raced to the marquee, which was set up in a
beautiful part of the English countryside.

The final of **Cook Off** was live, and beamed all over
the world.

"IT'S TIME TO COOK!"

announced Tony Truffle,
and the three finalists got to work.

Henry Heft was making a panettone, while Vivienne Vinegar was going to boil yet another egg.

"How is that an **Italian** dish, Miss Vinegar?" asked Tony.

"The hen who laid it was **Italian,**" claimed Vivienne.

And they were **off!** They had just half an hour to cook something delicious and *WOW* the judges.

All was going well for Ping Pong. She fried the mushrooms, added them to the creamy pasta sauce and added that to the spaghetti she had boiled perfectly. Not too hard. Not too soft. Just right.

The finishing touch was to be the Parmesan cheese she would grate on top, just to add that *WOW* factor. She took out the cheese grater and smiled to herself. She had very nearly done it. However, when Ping reached into her bag to grab the Parmesan cheese, she was *horrified* to discover a

BLOCK OF LARD.

"DAD!" she shouted across the marquee. Her proud parents had been peeping through a gap in the tent, and now dashed over to her.

"What's the matter, my love?" asked her mum.

"LOOK!" exclaimed the girl, showing them the lard.

"You picked up the wrong one, Peter!" chided Mum.

"It wasn't my fault! I had something in my eye," he protested.

"You had your own stink in your eye, Dad!"

"ONE MINUTE TO GO, COOKS!"

announced Tony Truffle.

"NO!" cried Ping. "My dish is ruined. I'll never win now!"

Peter Pong pinged!

PING!

"I have an idea!" he said brightly. "I know where we can get some MAGNIFICENT cheese!"

"There isn't time!" hissed Ping.

"THIRTY SECONDS TO GO!"

called out Truffle.

"SEE!" said the girl.

"Don't worry! Dad will save the day!" said Peter, and he grabbed a bowl and the cheese grater and dashed out of the marquee.

What he did next will give you NIGHTMARES. Not just NIGHTMARES, but CHEESY NIGHTMARES. And CHEESY NIGHTMARES are the worst.

Peter Pong kicked off his sandals and began grating the hard skin on the bottom of his feet into the bowl. *SCRAPE! SCRAPE! SCRAPE!* The pong was **phantasmapongagorical**.*

* The **Walliams*ictionary** has this too, so please buy one today. It is so much better than a real dictionary, which doesn't have any made-up words.

"TEN SECONDS TO GO!" Peter heard Tony Truffle announce from inside the tent.

As the final countdown began, he dashed back over to his daughter.

"TEN, NINE, EIGHT, SEVEN, SIX, FIVE, FOUR, THREE, TWO..."

Peter was in such a hurry that he tripped over a cooking pot and went flying. The **foot cheese** flew through the air, and before Ping could give it a sniff it sprinkled itself all over her pasta dish.

"ONE!" said Tony Truffle. "THAT IS IT, COOKS! Now is the moment of truth. Judges, it's TIME TO TASTE!"

The two judges, Boby Bollywood and Dame Penelope Plum, sprang into action. First, they tasted Heft's panettone cake.

"One most definitely **approves!**" announced the dame, taking a slice.

"Beautiful!" said Boby, stuffing his face with all that was left. "Like me!" The dame rolled her eyes. It was clear she hated how this hog hogged the camera.

Ping sniffed the **cheese** on her dish. It smelled **BAD.**

"Where did you get that cheese, Dad?" she hissed.

"Don't worry. It

was completely fresh!" he replied.

Meanwhile, the presenter and judges moved on to Vivienne Vinegar, who, as usual, did not crack a smile.

The dame was first to take a spoonful. "Mmm. One must congratulate you. A textbook egg-flavoured and egg-shaped egg. In a word, **eggy!**"

"It is definitely an **egg!**" muttered Tony.

Perfect! added Boby. "Just like me!" He popped the rest of the egg in his mouth all at once, shell and all.

The dame muttered "ridiculous little man" under her breath.

"DAD!" hissed Ping. "Is this cheese what I think it is?"

"Peter! No!" added Mum.

"*Shush!*" shushed Dad. "They won't notice a thing!"

The three arrived at Ping Pong's station.

"Wow!" remarked Tony. "The aroma of that cheese is...

overpowering!"

"It is Parmesan!" lied Peter. "It is a special type of *Italian cheese.*"

The presenter was most put out. "I think I know my cheese!" he snapped, patting his round tummy.

Tony, Boby Bollywood and the dame all eagerly helped themselves to the spaghetti.

"I'm starving!" announced Tony.

"Ravenous!" added the dame.

"So hungry I am angry," exclaimed Boby, who still had bits of the cake and egg on his face.

"HANGRY!"

At once, they all tucked into Ping Pong's pasta. The poor girl looked on in **HORROR**, sure she was about to see her dreams dashed. But, as soon as Tony, Boby and the dame began scoffing, it was clear they were enjoying it immensely!

"SCRUMPTIOUS!"

declared Tony.

"The three Ds," began the dame. "Delightful, delectable and delicious!"

"YUMMY!" was Boby's verdict. There wasn't much left, so he picked up the bowl, and poured the remainder down his throat.

"Do we have a winner?" pressed the presenter.

A hush descended upon the marquee. A hush that could be heard all around the world.

The two judges whispered to each other.

"Yes! We do!" announced the dame.

All three contestants – Henry Heft, Vivienne Vinegar and, of course, Ping Pong – looked on nervously. Who would be crowned *Cook of Cooks?* Ping's parents put their hands together in prayer. Might Peter's **foot cheese** have turned his daughter's pasta dish into a

TASTE SENSATION?

Who... who... WHO would be the winner?

The world was watching.

And waiting.

This was the most *thrilling* piece of television since man first set foot on the moon. And just as important.

If not more so.

In fact, definitely more so.

The two judges whispered into Tony Truffle's ear, before the presenter cleared his throat.

"The winner of **Cook Off** this year," he began, "and *Cook of Cooks*, is..."

Then he left a pause so long you could read the whole of *The Lord of the Rings* while waiting for it to finish.

"PING PONG!"

"YES!"

screamed
Peter Pong.

"HURRAH!"

screamed
his wife.

"I CAN'T BELIEVE IT!" exclaimed Ping.

"Well, do believe it," continued Tony Truffle, "because you, young lady, have beaten the grown-ups!"

Henry Heft growled, "GRRR!"

Vivienne Vinegar gave the girl a stare so powerful it could fry an egg.

The two judges brought out the trophy, a gold frying pan, and handed it to Ping.

"Congratulations!"

"Well done!" they cooed.

"It was my secret ingredient that swung it!" piped up Peter.

"SHUSH!" shushed Ping.

"Secret ingredient?" asked Tony Truffle. "Do tell!"

"No, don't tell, Dad!" pleaded the girl.

Now everyone wanted to know, the judges, the other finalists...

"WHAT SECRET INGREDIENT?"

"TELL US WHAT IT IS, MAN!"

"WE NEED TO KNOW!"

"WAS IT A BOILED EGG?"

"Well," began Peter, "if you must know, that wasn't Parmesan cheese, it was—"

"DAD, NO!" screamed Ping.

"FOOT CHEESE!" he announced proudly.

"LOOK!" And with that he showed off his rancid smelly feet.

Suddenly Tony Truffle, Boby Bollywood and Dame Penelope Plum all turned a violent shade of green.

Tony Truffle was first.

He hurled his spaghetti over Boby Bollywood.

"BLEURGH!"

Boby was not far behind. He hurled his spaghetti all over the dame.

"BLLEEUURRGGHH!"

It may surprise you to know that of the three the dame

"BLLLLLLLLLEEEEEEEEEEUUUUUUUU

could hurl the furthest.

The elderly lady hurled her spaghetti all over the Pong family.

"YUCK!"

Then she hurled spaghetti over Henry Heft, who burst into tears.

"BOO! HOO!"

Then she hurled spaghetti over Vivienne Vinegar, whose eyes bulged out of her head like two poached eggs.

Then the dame hurled spaghetti over Tony Truffle, blowing his wig clean off.

WHOOSH!

"I never knew I was bald!" he lied. Spaghetti sat on his bald head where his wig had been.

RRRRRRRRRRRGGGGGGGGGHHHHHHHHHH!"

And, finally, she turned to Boby Bollywood.

"OH NO!" he screamed. "THINK OF MY FANS!"

"Oh yes," the dame replied, before hurling spaghetti all over her fellow judge.

"BLLLLLLLEEEEEEEEUUUUUU

Boby jolted back to try to dodge the spray. He **whacked** into one of the posts holding up the marquee.

BOSH!

At once the whole thing wobbled.

WOBBLE! WUBBLE! WIBBLE!

And crashed to the ground.

THUD!

The cameras kept rolling as millions of viewers around the world witnessed the **carnage** from the comfort of their living rooms.

"D-A-D!" screamed Ping. "YOU **RUINED** IT FOR ME!"

"What was the problem?" he asked. **"Did it need more cheese?"**

BELINDA BRAG

BELLE WAS A LITTLE GIRL with a big problem.

Her **mother.**

Belinda saw her daughter, Belle, as a miniature version of her. Belinda would do the little girl's hair in a huge do like hers, dress her up in a bright pink dress just like hers and even put a string of pearls on her, just like hers.

Poor Belle ended up looking like mini-Mum.

In fact, if you looked at the pair, with Belinda standing a few paces behind Belle, you might think they were identical.*

The problem was that Belle didn't want to be like her mother. She wanted to be herself. As soon as her mother's back was turned, she shook down her hair, pulled off her pearls and whipped off her dress to reveal a T-shirt and denim shorts underneath.

Now that Belle looked like herself, Belle felt like herself.

* **WALLYFACT:** This is something I invented called "perspective".

Despite being sent to the poshest girls' school in the country, **LADY HAUGHTY'S SCHOOL FOR YOUNG LADIES**, Belle loved doing things like:

Standing in **puddles**

Making **mud pies**

Climbing **trees**

Running through tall grass

Digging for worms

Playing **conkers**

Chasing **pigeons**

Skimming stones

Rolling down *hills*

Being dragged through a **HEDGE** backwards

Every afternoon when Belle trudged out of **HAUGHTY'S SCHOOL,** she would go bright red with embarrassment at seeing what her mother had on that day:

A **fake fur coat** in the height of summer…

Sparkly diamond earrings with gems so big and heavy her earlobes dropped down to her bottom…

Designer sunglasses spotted with rubies…

A **ballgown** with a train as long as a football pitch…

A **mock crocodile-skin handbag** over her wrist that was so large you could fit an actual crocodile in it…

Oh, Mum, no! thought the girl.

As she paced nearer and nearer to the school gates, Belle could hear her mother holding court with all the other parents waiting for their *little princesses.* Belinda would **brag** and **brag** and **brag.** Each day of the week she would make up some fresh nonsense.

'I took my Belle out of Sports Day because I didn't feel it was fair on all your girls. I am sorry to say my Belle would win every single race!'

she boasted one Monday.

"M-U-M!" bawled Belle, desperate for her to stop, going as red as a tomato.

"My Belle is only twelve, but all the teachers say she is a genius. She could go straight to university, but it just wouldn't be fair on the students there – she would show them all up!"

Belinda boasted on Tuesday.

"NOOOO! STOP!" pleaded her daughter, going as red as a post box.

"In the school pantomime, I know they wanted my Belle to play every single role. But I said to the Drama mistress, 'No! Please, please, please give the other much less talented children a chance!'"

was Wednesday's boast.

"PLEASE, MUM, NO!"

"Of course, my Belle can speak a hundred languages. She can even speak languages that haven't been invented yet."

This was on Thursday.

"MUM! THIS IS SOOOOOOOOOOOO EMBARRASSING!" Belle was now going as red as a red ant. But Belinda had saved the worst until last. Step forward,

Friday…

"It's not easy for my Belle being by far the most beautiful girl in the school. Everyone says she gets it from her mother, but that's not for me to say! But she does. I am so desperately sad that all your little girls are such monsters. Have you ever thought of sending them to school with paper bags over their heads? It might help them feel better! Poor hideous little wretches!"

"ENOUGH IS ENOUGH!" exclaimed Belle. Her face was now as bright red as a London bus.

So far, so bad.

Until, one day, a girl arrived at HAUGHTY'S SCHOOL with a mother even worse than Belinda.

Yes, the impossible became true.

The mother's name was Camilla Crow, and she never, ever, ever stopped crowing about her daughter, Carol. It was strange, as Carol was the most gormless girl you could ever meet. She never spoke, unless in grunts.

"HUH?"

Carol seemed content to spend the entire day either picking her nose or scratching her bottom.

PICK!

SCRATCH!

49

That was as thrilling as life got for Carol. But, but, BUT, if you listened to her mother, then **oh my goodness!** This nose-picking, bottom-scratching little grunter was a **LIVING LEGEND!**

According to Camilla, her daughter, Carol, had:

Been an Olympic **gold-medal-winning** gymnast when she was still a baby...

Made the record books as the youngest **bestselling author,** who published an autobiography at the age of four called *Little Me, Big Dreams*...

Single-handedly saved the **Amazonian rainforest** by releasing a charity single called 'Wee on a Tree (If It's on Fire)'...

Built her **own rocket** and **ZOOMED** to Mars, but forgot to take any pictures while she was there...

Invented a new kind of fruit that she called the **"RINKADINKYDODDLEBERRY"...**

Made **world peace** a reality at last, though sadly for only one minute...

Taught her goldfish to play **SCRABBLE...**

Made a model of the Eiffel Tower out of matchsticks, which was exactly the same height as the real Eiffel Tower...

Learned to juggle seventeen gerbils at once...*
Invented the FLOP-FLIP, a revolutionary new flip-flop that
FLOPS before it FLIPS...

Translated all the Harry Potter books into Chinese,
and then back again into English...Won first prize in a
bottom-scratching competition...

Only the last one seemed likely. Still, that didn't
stop Camilla Crow crowing at the school gates every
afternoon about her Carol.

Belle felt sorry for Carol. Carol's mother was even
worse than hers.

It soon became a

WAR OF THE MOTHERS.

Carol Crow's crowing
enraged Belinda Brag.
The pair became locked in
a battle – a battle to outdo one
another with boasts about their
daughters.

One afternoon, as the girls were all pouring
out of the school, things turned UGLY...

* **WALLYFACT:** The world record for juggling gerbils is held by the Russian
Igor Igorski. Igor once juggled nineteen gerbils at once. But as he has
three arms many gerbil jugglers consider this an unfair advantage.

It all started when Belinda began with, "On the school trip to the zoo, my Belle saved her entire class from being eaten by a hungry crocodile. Fortunately, my daughter distracted the beast by reciting some poetry. In ancient Greek."

Camilla was not to be outdone. She fired back with, "That's nothing. Just the other day, a grizzly bear burst into the playground. Luckily my Carol wrestled it to the ground with one hand just before it could take a bite out of the headmistress."

All their two daughters could do was stop and stare at the HORROR that was unfolding.

"Your Carol couldn't wrestle a grizzly bear!" sneered Belinda.

"Why ever not?" snapped Camilla.

"Because your gormless girl is far too busy picking her nose and scratching her – and I hate to say this, as I am a lady of class and distinction – her behind region!"

"I think she means you," muttered Belle to Carol.

"How dare you?" exclaimed Camilla. "My Carol has never scratched her bottom in her entire life!"

"HUH!" grunted Carol, which Belle took to mean: "Yes, I have, you muppet!"

"All that vile little thing does is go from picking her nose to scratching her... ahem... *bottom!*"

"All right! I admit it! But at least my Carol uses different hands for each task! Unlike your disgusting little daughter who uses the same one! **DISGUSTING!**"

"Ouch!" hissed Belle to Carol. "That was a low blow from your mum. True, though."

"HUH!" agreed the gormless girl.

The two mothers were now nose job to nose job.

"GRRR!"

"GRRR!"

"Come on!" said Belle.

"We'd better drag our mothers away before a brawl breaks out!"

Carol shrugged. **"HUH!"**

So Belle grabbed her mum's hand. "Come along now, Mother!"

And Carol grabbed her mum's arm. **"HUH!"**

Then they dragged them off in opposite directions towards their Rolls-Royces. The Brag family had an electric-blue Rolls-Royce. But the Crow family had an even more revolting one in shocking pink.*

Then the two mothers raced each other along the roads back home.

BRUMM! ZOOM!

Once at their respective country houses, Belinda and Camilla could seethe in peace. And seethe they did. They seethed all afternoon. They seethed all evening. And they seethed through the night. By the morning they were seething more than ever. Bad luck that it was the HAUGHTY'S SCHOOL Sports Day, a once-yearly occasion when all the parents spent an afternoon cheering on their daughters in running races and the like. Of course, winning meant infinitely more to the parents than it did to the girls.

* WALLYFACT: The worst colour for any car is BOTTOM-BURP BROWN.

LADY HAUGHTY'S SCHOOL FOR YOUNG LADIES
SPORTS DAY

The first event of the afternoon was the hurdles.

Belinda Brag and Camilla Crow bustled into their places at the finish line. Treating Sports Day like a fashion parade, Belinda was in a lime-green dress, and Camilla in a luminous yellow one. Seething more than ever, the pair lowered their sunglasses to shoot each other evil stares.

Meanwhile, their daughters took their places at the start line with the other more eager-looking girls. Belle couldn't give a stuff about winning. She knew she wasn't the fastest or the strongest, and didn't mind one bit. The girl was good at other things, like standing in puddles.

"You can win this, Belle!" called out Belinda.

"No, I can't, but whatever!" she called back.

"Do it for Mama!"

"Now I really want to come last," the girl muttered to herself.

"Beat them, Carol!" bawled Camilla.

"Beat them all! Show them that

you are the best of the best! They must bow before the might and majesty of Miss Carol Crow!"

"**HUH?**" grunted Carol, who was actually facing the wrong way.

BANG! went the starting pistol.

As all the other girls raced off, Belle and Carol were immediately joint last. Neither picked up enough speed to leap over the first hurdle, so...

CLUNK! CLUNK!

...they just knocked them over instead.

And the next one.

CLUNK! CLUNK!

And the next!

CLUNK! CLUNK!

Both warring mothers looked as if they were going to explode with rage.

"BELLE! RUN! JUMP!"

"CAROL! MOVE YOUR BLASTED BOTTOM!"

But neither girl did. In fact, Belle became distracted by something on the ground.

"LOOK!" she exclaimed. "A WORM!"

She picked up the wiggly-waggly thing, before waving it under Carol's nose.

"HUH!" said Carol, which Belle took to mean "I like your worm". The girl then picked her nose and wiped the bogey on a hurdle.

"YOUR BELLE IS RUINING IT FOR MY CAROL WITH HER REVOLTING WORM!"

bellowed Camilla.

"YOUR CAROL IS DISTRACTING MY BELLE BY PICKING A PARTICULARLY LARGE BOOGER!"

bawled Belinda.

"WELL, YOU WOULD KNOW ALL ABOUT BIG BOOGERS BECAUSE YOU LOOK LIKE ONE!"

Camilla had a point. Belinda's dress was bogey green.

"I'VE HAD QUITE ENOUGH OF YOU, BELINDA BRAG!"

"AND I'VE HAD QUITE ENOUGH OF YOU, CAMILLA CROW!"

With that, Belinda Brag stomped over to the pole vault and seized one of the long poles.

Meanwhile, Camilla snatched a javelin. In no time, the pair were locked in a deadly duel.

"TAKE THAT!" snarled Belinda, swooshing her pole.

"TAKE THIS!" snapped Camilla, swishing her javelin.

CLANK! CLINK! CLANK! went the weapons, as they bashed together.

Belinda yanked up her pole, hitting some of the other parents on their heads as she did so.

CLONK! **DONK!** BONK!

"OUCH!"

"OW!"

"OWEE!"

Meanwhile, wrenching back her javelin, Camilla managed to whack all the others.

THWACK! **THWUCK!** **THWOCK!**

"ARGH!"

"OOWW!"

"URGH!"

Soon, all the posh parents were arming themselves to join in the fight. Everything on the sports field became a weapon. Shotputs. Discuses. Even sand from the long jump was thrown in faces. At one point, the HAUGHTY'S SCHOOL headmistress herself, Miss Prunella Prim, was hoisted up by some of the mothers and used as a battering ram against a cowering huddle of fathers.

"HELP!"

The school Sports Day had descended into a gladiator battle. It was posh parent against posh parent.

And they fought DIRTY.

There was:

hair-pulling

arm-pinching

leg-scratching

finger-bending

nose-yanking

eye-poking

toe-stamping

ear-flicking

elbow-tickling

head-locking

even
BOTTOM-BITING!

"URGH!"

"ARGH!" "OW!"

BOOM!

POW! KERUNCH!

Soon the playing field was a swirling mass of gruesome grown-ups. The girls all stared open-mouthed in shock as their parents bashed and bawled at each other.

"YOUR DAUGHTER HAS A WONKY FRINGE!"

"YOUR DAUGHTER LOOKS LIKE A GUINEA PIG!"

"YOUR DAUGHTER STINKS OF TURNIPS!"

Still holding the worm, Belle shouted over the din, "GIRLS! WHO THINKS OUR MUMS AND DADS ARE A BUNCH OF FRUITCAKES?"

The girls all cheered in agreement. "HURRAH!"

None cheered louder than sisters Sophie and Anna, whose mother was yanking the nostril hair of one of the fathers.

"ARGH!"

"SO, WHO FANCIES BUNKING OFF SPORTS DAY AND BEING DRAGGED THROUGH A HEDGE BACKWARDS INSTEAD?" called out Belle.

This was the girl's second-favourite thing. After standing in a puddle, of course.

"YES!" cried all the girls, except Carol. Carol grunted, **"HUH!"** which Belle took to mean "yes".

In no time, the girls were having a whale of a time. Laughing, joking, climbing trees, skipping through the fields and making up games. And, best of all, picking their noses and scratching their bottoms to their hearts' content. Preferably with the same hand.

The girls were being happy being themselves,
while their parents made absolute
fools of themselves.

BARRY
BOVVER

To say Barry Bovver looked like King Kong would
be unkind to King Kong. This beast of a man had:

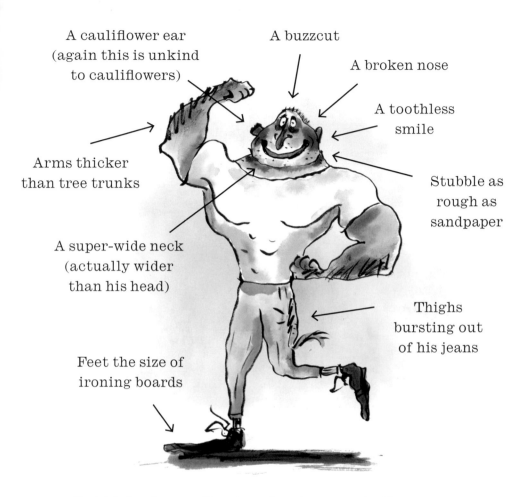

A cauliflower ear (again this is unkind to cauliflowers)

A buzzcut

A broken nose

A toothless smile

Arms thicker than tree trunks

Stubble as rough as sandpaper

A super-wide neck (actually wider than his head)

Thighs bursting out of his jeans

Feet the size of ironing boards

But his brain was the size of a ping-pong ball. Whenever he was called upon to use it, such as when asked to spell his own name, he would cry, **"MY BRAIN HURTS!"**

Fortunately, most of the time Barry Bovver didn't have to use his brain. That's because his job was all about how big his muscles were. Barry was a **strongman**. He competed with other strongmen all over the country to see who was the **strongest strongman** of them all.

In these contests, the strongmen would:

Pull a tree out of the ground YANK!

"OI! PUT THIS BUS DOWN! I AM TRYING TO GET TO WORK!"

Wrestle a rhinoceros "MOO!"

Lift a double-decker bus above their heads

Run a race with a fridge-freezer strapped to their back "GRUNT!"

Eat a tank "BURP!"

Perform a squat-lift, holding a walrus "HOOT!"

Do a staring competition with a hamster NIBBLE!

Snap a train carriage in half KERUNCH!

Flip a fire engine over SMASH!

Do a tug-of-war with an aeroplane as it tries to take off

"EXCUSE ME! I AM TRYING TO GO ON HOLIDAY. WILL YOU PLEASE LET GO?"

BARRY BOVVER

Just like Barry, all the other famous strongmen looked as if they'd been **inflated.**
There was:

Micky Might: famous for competing in only a pair of very tight red underpants.

Chaz Carnage: he ate a shark for breakfast.

Vince Vicious: legend has it he once head-butted a house, and the house crumbled to the ground.

MUNGO MUSCLE: he only worked out his top half so he had the biggest chest and arms and the smallest spindliest legs.

The Ogre: he only spoke in grunts. From both ends.

PETE PUNCH: he could punch a hole in concrete, and often would.

Gunter Girth: he was so wide he couldn't fit through any door.

Dick Dense: famous for being the cleverest of the strongmen, as he once got a C in Pottery.

Thunder Thump: his fists were bigger than his head.

And the one strongwoman, **Cloris Clout:** she was the most terrifying of them all. Cloris could lift all the strongmen with one hand. And an elephant in the other.

Whenever Barry entered one of these strongmen competitions, which happened most weekends at **FUNFAIRS** and in pub car parks, his family had to come too: his wife, Bianca, and their daughter, Brian.

I know what you are thinking: who would call their daughter **Brian?**

Barry Bovver, that's who. The man didn't realise that Brian was a boy's name.

"MY BRAIN HURTS!"

he exclaimed whenever anyone asked about this.

Needless to say, it was hard being a girl named Brian. But nothing was as hard as having Barry Bovver for a father...

If the family went for a picnic and were sitting in the shade, Dad would rip up the tree and move it somewhere else. *RIIIIIIIIIIIP!*

When Mum served up an entire roast hog for Sunday lunch, Dad would eat the whole thing in one gulp.

"BURP!"

If there wasn't any room in the supermarket car park, Dad would free up a space by lifting a parked car and placing it right on top of another. *CRUNCH!*

When the school bus left one morning without his daughter, Dad yanked it back to the bus stop.

SCREECH!

Once, Dad leaped on to a bouncy castle at Brian's birthday party, and all the children were bounced miles into the air.*

WHOOSH!

If Brian got low marks in a test, Dad would storm into school and swing the teacher around by their ankles until his daughter was made top of the class.

"YES! IT'S AN A+ NOW, MR BOVVER! PLEASE, PLEASE, PLEASE, I BEG YOU, LET ME GO!"

WHIRR!

Whenever Barry went to the loo, he yanked the chain on the toilet so hard that he would bring the bathroom ceiling down with it.

CRUMBLE!

CRASH!

CLATTER!

* **WALLYFACT:** They are still waiting for one of the children to come back down. At the time of writing, a boy named Leo is just re-entering the Earth's atmosphere.

BARRY BOVVER

When Father Christmas didn't give Brian a nice enough present, Barry Bovver lifted up the grotto, complete with Father Christmas, reindeer and elves, high into the air until he did.

"HO! HO! H-H-HELP!"

If there was no food in the house, Dad might pull a brick out of the wall and snack on that.*

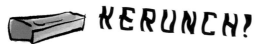 **KERUNCH!**

Christmas dinner was always an ordeal, as poor Granny would be yanked across the room and fly out of the window if she dared to pull a cracker with her son.

"A A A H H H !"

 **CRASH!**

Sadly, Barry Bovver was not the brightest spark. So Brian soon learned it was best not to tell her father when something went wrong, or he was likely to respond not with brains but with BRUTE FORCE.

* **WALLYFACT:** Bricks are not tasty. If you do find yourself having to eat one, do smother on some jam or peanut butter. Though, I warn you, bricks will still taste rather "bricky".

One afternoon, the girl returned home from school in floods of tears.

"Brian, my darlin'!" exclaimed her mother. "What's the matter?"

Before she spoke, the girl looked through the kitchen window into their little garden.

There she could see her father weightlifting. He had a long metal pole with a caravan on each end. Barry was pushing them up and down as he counted his repetitions.

"A million and five, a million and six..."

It was safe. He couldn't hear. So the girl continued.

"Oh, Mum, it was the headmistress! She accused me of cheating in the exam!"

"Did you?" asked Mum.

"Of course not!" exclaimed the girl. "It was this boy, Swifty Swindle, who cheated by copying me! He is always doing that and getting away with it!"

"That's awful! I need to have a word with that woman!"

"If you could, Mum," said the girl, dabbing her eyes. "But promise you won't tell Dad!"

Before Mum had a chance to answer, a huge face loomed at the kitchen window.

"DON'T TELL DAD WOT?" It was Barry Bovver and, judging by his expression, he was in a bovver.

"Nothing, Dad," lied his daughter.

"Go back to your weightlifting, Barry," urged his wife. "You've still got another million reps to go!"

But Barry was not going to give this up. "Someone's upset my little princess. Brian? Tell me. Who done this?"

"Brian! Don't tell him it was the headmistress!" blurted Bianca. Mum was not the brightest spark either.

"MUM!" exclaimed Brian. "You've gone and done it now!"

"Sorry, love!" she muttered.

"I'm going to give that headmistress a piece of my mind!" Barry declared, stomping into the kitchen.

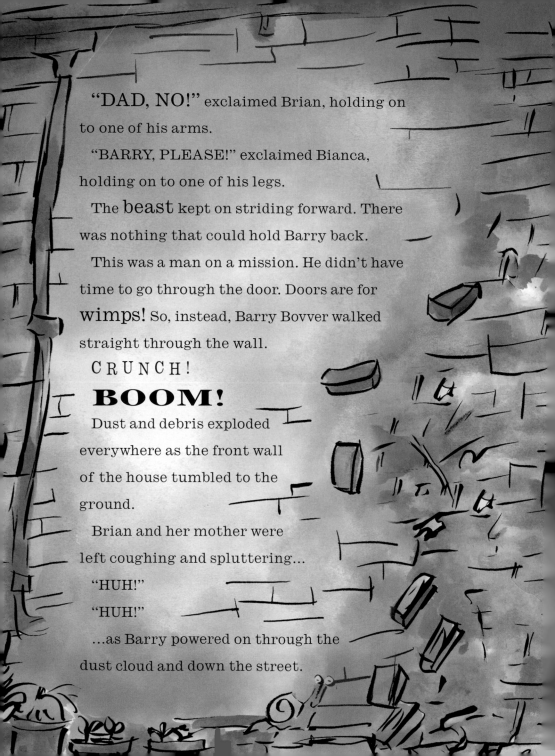

"DAD, NO!" exclaimed Brian, holding on to one of his arms.

"BARRY, PLEASE!" exclaimed Bianca, holding on to one of his legs.

The beast kept on striding forward. There was nothing that could hold Barry back.

This was a man on a mission. He didn't have time to go through the door. Doors are for wimps! So, instead, Barry Bovver walked straight through the wall.

C R U N C H !

BOOM!

Dust and debris exploded everywhere as the front wall of the house tumbled to the ground.

Brian and her mother were left coughing and spluttering…

"HUH!"

"HUH!"

…as Barry powered on through the dust cloud and down the street.

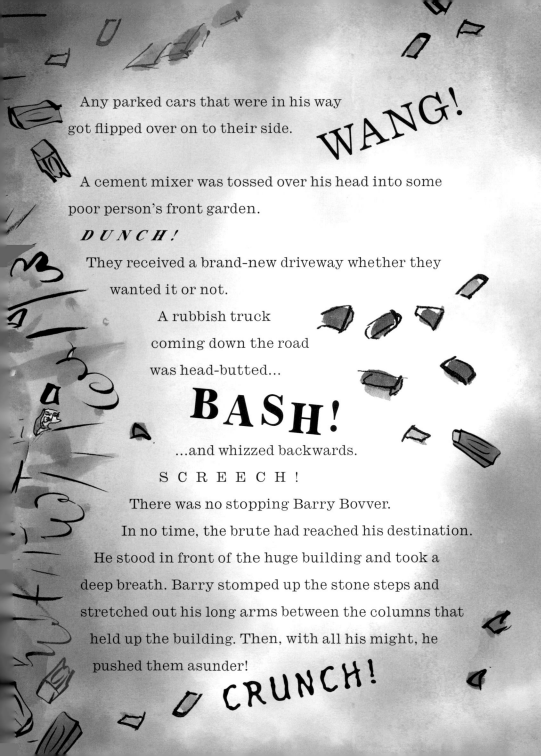

Any parked cars that were in his way got flipped over on to their side. **WANG!**

A cement mixer was tossed over his head into some poor person's front garden.

DUNCH!

They received a brand-new driveway whether they wanted it or not.

A rubbish truck coming down the road was head-butted…

BASH!

…and whizzed backwards.

S C R E E C H !

There was no stopping Barry Bovver.

In no time, the brute had reached his destination. He stood in front of the huge building and took a deep breath. Barry stomped up the stone steps and stretched out his long arms between the columns that held up the building. Then, with all his might, he pushed them asunder!

CRUNCH!

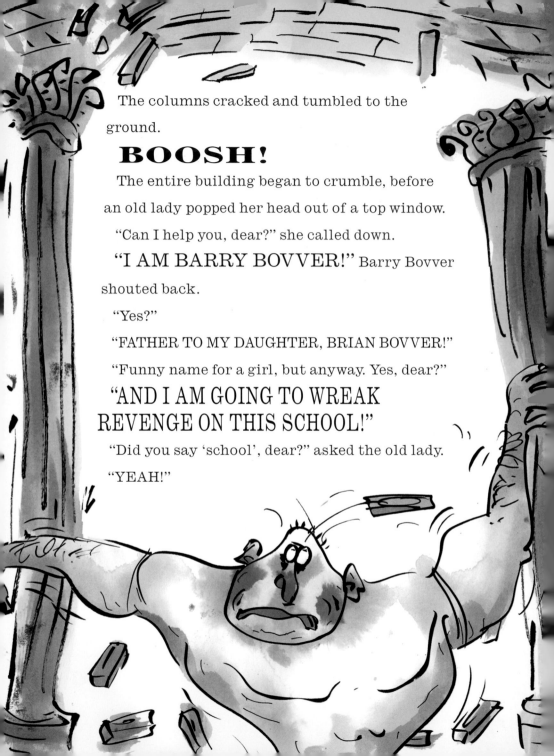

The columns cracked and tumbled to the ground.

BOOSH!

The entire building began to crumble, before an old lady popped her head out of a top window.

"Can I help you, dear?" she called down.

"I AM BARRY BOVVER!" Barry Bovver shouted back.

"Yes?"

"FATHER TO MY DAUGHTER, BRIAN BOVVER!"

"Funny name for a girl, but anyway. Yes, dear?"

"AND I AM GOING TO WREAK REVENGE ON THIS SCHOOL!"

"Did you say 'school', dear?" asked the old lady.

"YEAH!"

"This isn't the school, dear," she replied. "This is the old folks' home. The school is right next door."

This stopped Barry in his tracks.

"MY BRAIN HURTS!" he exclaimed.

"Easy mistake to make. We are always getting their post. School is just there, dear!"

"SORRY! AND THANK YOU!"

"Have a nice day, dear!" added the old lady as the front wall of the building tumbled to the ground.

CRASH! WALLOP! BANG!

All the old folks were revealed in their rooms, cooing at Barry Bovver's remodelling of their home.

"Ooh, what a lovely view!"

"Nice to have some fresh air!"

"Is it time for tea?"

Meanwhile, Barry Bovver stomped off next door. To be completely sure he was in the right place, Barry shouted up at the building.

"HEADMISTRESS?"

After a moment, a proper-looking lady popped her head out of her office window.

"School is closed!" she barked, patting her hairdo.

"I AM BARRY BOVVER!" he shouted up. "MY DAUGHTER BRIAN BOVVER'S DAD!"

"Peculiar name for a girl, but do go on!"

"MY PRINCESS IS IN TEARS. POOR PRINCESS BRIAN. SHE NEVER CHEATED IN NO TEST!"

"Yes, I am so, so sorry. Apologies! Apologies! I made a mistake! It was Swifty Swindle all along. The boy has been put in detention. I just telephoned your home, but there was no answer!"

"THE FRONT WALL CAVED IN!"

"Oh dear. I am sorry to hear that! Now, I must dash home to catch some cartoons before tea. So I do pray this is the end of the matter!"

"NO, IT IS NOT!" raged Barry. "I AM GOING TO TEACH THIS SCHOOL A LESSON!"

"We do the teaching here, thank you, Mr Bovver," replied the headmistress.

"DON'T YOU MAKE A MUG OUT OF ME! THE SCHOOL IS FOR IT!"

With that, the beast of a man leaned down, and wedged his mighty sausage fingers underneath the building.

"DAD! STOP!" shouted a breathless Brian, who had just made it to the school gates with her mother. Both were coated from head to toe in dust.

"BARRY! PLEASE! THINK!" added Bianca.

"I DON'T FINK! IT MAKES MY BRAIN HURT! I USE MY MUSCLES!" he boomed. "NOW STAND BACK!"

Then, after a considerable amount of huffing and puffing, he lifted the entire school building off the ground.

"OOF!"

"PUT THIS SCHOOL DOWN AT ONCE!" ordered the

headmistress. "OR I WILL PUT YOU IN DETENTION TOO! YOU CAN WRITE OUT A HUNDRED LINES: 'I MUST NOT LIFT THE SCHOOL BUILDING OFF THE GROUND!'"

"NO!" shouted Barry.

"I AM NOT DOING NO DETENTION! I'M GONNA PUT THIS SCHOOL WHERE IT BELONGS! IN THE BIN!"

Holding the entire weight of the school building with his arms, he staggered across the playground to the wheelie bins in the corner.

"HUH! HUH! HUH!" he exclaimed

in effort. The school was heavy! A thousand times heavier than two caravans.

"I DON'T THINK IT'S GOING TO FIT, DAD!" shouted Brian.

Her father was really straining with the weight now. Beads of sweat as big as tennis balls were pouring down his face. He looked up at the huge school building, then down at the not-so-big bins. Even Barry Bovver could see this wasn't going to work.

"DO YOU HAVE ANY BIGGER BINS?" he called up to the headmistress, who was clinging on to the window frame for dear life.

"NOOOO!" she wailed. "NOW PUT THE SCHOOL DOWN THIS INSTANT!"

Barry went left, then right, and then the entire school building began wobbling.

"PLEASE, DAD! DO AS THE HEADMISTRESS SAYS!" called Brian.

Now the beads of sweat were the size of footballs.

"I DON'T THINK I CAN HOLD IT ANY..."

But before Barry could say "LONGER" he lost his grip and the school came crashing down upon him.

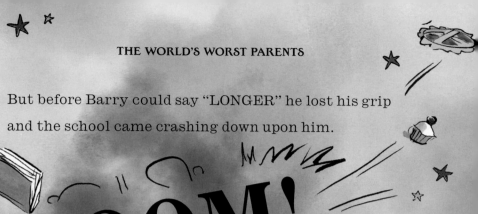

BOOM!
SPLAT!

"DAD!" called Brian as her horrified mum held her tight.

There was no way they could lift the school building, however hard they tried.

"IS HE ALL RIGHT?" hollered the headmistress.

"NO! HE IS NOT! CALL AN AMBULANCE! CALL THE FIRE BRIGADE! CALL THE POLICE!" bawled Bianca.

"I know!" exclaimed Brian. "Let's call the strongmen!"

That's exactly what they did, and in no time the nine strongmen and one strongwoman had arrived.

Micky Might (dressed only in his tight red underpants), **Chaz Carnage**, Vince Vicious, MUNGO MUSCLE, the ogre, PETE PUNCH, Gunter Girth, Dick Dense, Thunder Thump and Cloris Clout all rushed to the scene. Once they were all there, they gathered around the school building, and placed their sausage fingers beneath it.

"HEAVE!" called Brian, and the ten strong-people lifted the school high into the air. Underneath, their comrade Barry Bovver was lying there as flat as a pancake. They put the school building down on to the playground.

SHONT!

Brian and Bianca rushed over to him.

"DAD! DAD! Are you OK?" gushed his tearful daughter.

"Sorry, Brian. I fink the school was just a tiny bit too heavy for me!"

NEE-NAW! NEE-NAW!

An ambulance sped into the playground. The doctors rolled Brian Bovver up like a French-style crêpe so they could fit him in the back of the ambulance.

"Is he going to be all right?" asked Brian.

"We should be able to knead him back into shape," replied the doctor. "I hope his brain hasn't been damaged in some way."

"I don't think there is any chance of that," replied the girl.

Just as the ambulance doors were about to close, Barry the crêpe sat up from the stretcher, and addressed his fellow strong-people.

"I know I am not the brightest spark," he began, "but I hope I have taught you all an important lesson today…"

"What?"

"Do tell us!"

"We wanna know!" replied all the strong-people.

"I may not be the brightest spark, but remember this. Never try to lift a school building above your head!" declared Barry.

There was silence for a moment before all the strongmen and one strongwoman broke into applause.

Brian smiled. **"You will always be my brightest spark, Dad. The brightest spark of light in my life."**

The man looked close to tears.

"Fanks. Next time I will try to use my brain!" he said, pointing to his chest.

Brian didn't have the heart to tell him his brain was actually in his head.

And as the ambulance doors closed,
Barry Bovver smiled and waved goodbye
with his huge flat hand.

POSY POOCH

The mother who loved her dog much more than her child

POSY POOCH

POSY POOCH WAS BARKING mad about dogs. She always wore bright woolly jumpers and leggings with pictures of puppies on them, finished off with doggy slippers. These were huge furry monstrosities shaped like St Bernards, and nearly as big as the real thing.

Her look was topped off with a hairband that had dog ears sticking out of the top.

In the highly unlikely event that you had somehow missed Posy Pooch's love of dogs, she had customised the family car. First, she covered it in thick brown carpet so it looked like fur. Next she stuck a ball of black foam to the bonnet for a nose. The finishing touches were all made of fabric: eyes, ears, a tail and even a big floppy tongue hanging from the front grille. Posy Pooch named the car "THE MUTT MOBILE".

The lady had named the family home **"POOCH PLACE"**.
It was a house themed entirely around dogs.
Posy had purchased:

Wallpaper of **Weimaraners**

Curtains adorned with **Chihuahuas**

A **Pekinese** plate set

A sofa in the shape of a **schnauzer**

Mugs with **Malteses** painted on them

A **chow-chow** coffee table

A **King Charles spaniel** kettle

Great Dane glasses

A **Rottweiler** rug

A bedspread of **basset hounds**

If that weren't enough, all the hedges in the front
lawn had been cut into the shapes of **poodles.** In the back
garden, she had a giant stone
statue of a **springer spaniel,** which
looked as if it were leaping into
the pond.

Posy had
just the one human
child. Her name was Peaches – *Peaches Pooch.*
From a very young age, her mother had
dressed Peaches up as a dog. This wasn't
just for fancy-dress parties. Oh no. The poor
girl had a wardrobe full of dog costumes
and was made to wear them for all kinds
of occasions.

A Boston terrier costume for a christening

A Dalmatian outfit for a dental appointment

A Border terrier suit for the school disco

A golden retriever get-up for the Girl Guides' summer fête

A collie costume for ballet practice

A Pomeranian get-up for a playdate

A bulldog outfit for a bar mitzvah

A red setter suit to go roller-skating in the park

A corgi costume for a school trip to Buckingham Palace

A pug outfit for a karaoke party

Needless to say, Peaches hated being dressed up like this, but she didn't have any choice. Her mother didn't buy her any other clothes. It meant all the children at school would make fun of her. Except one. Kitty Purr. Her mother was crazy about cats, so she had to go to school dressed as a white fluffy kitten.

Of course, Posy Pooch owned a dog. If her husband, Paul, hadn't been allergic to dogs (they made him itch and sneeze), she would have had a hundred. However, what she lacked in numbers, she made up for in size. Posy chose one of the biggest dog breeds in the world for her pet. A **Tibetan mastiff**.

The dog was named after the country from which it originated: Tibet, set in the Himalayan mountains, bordering China. Mastiffs are massive dogs with huge feet and drooping ears. This great lolloping thing was bred as a guard dog. It was the size of a grizzly bear and looked not unlike one too.

SPOT THE DIFFERENCE

DOG

BEAR

Posy named her dog **Nigel.** If ever there was a less suitable name for a dog, I would like to hear it. The mastiff looked absolutely nothing like a **Nigel.** But, like all names, it stuck.

Needless to say, Posy lavished love on her pooch. Whatever **Nigel** wanted, **Nigel** got:

A long relaxing bath twice a day, followed by a blow-dry

A string of sausages as a snack, on the hour, every hour

A silver-plated dog bowl the size of a paddling pool with the name **NIGEL** printed on it

A gold dog tag, with the words HELLO, MY NAME IS **NIGEL** on one side, and YES, I KNOW I AM BEAUTIFUL on the other

A luxury leather lead-and-collar set, designed by the famous fashion designer Barbara Barking

A one-hundred-piece grooming set for all **Nigel**'s needs

95

Dog toys made especially large so **Nigel** could play with them

A specially made dog basket, which was lined with only the softest silk bedding

A stuffed bunny toy he liked to hurl around the house that was too big to fit through a doorway

A ball that had a motor inside, operated by remote control as **Nigel** was too lazy to fetch it

A life-sized oil painting of **Nigel** that was given pride of place over the fireplace in the living room

The problem was that the dog was absolutely impossible to train. So **Nigel** ran **riot.** When Posy sent Peaches to take her precious **Nigel** out for a walk in the park, the poor girl would be dragged across the grass, clinging on to the lead for dear life.

"ARGH!"

If the Pooch family were having dinner, **Nigel** would wolf down everyone's food in one gulp, and poor Peaches would go hungry.

"CHOMP!"

Nigel took to sleeping in Posy and Paul's room. Peaches's mother would snuggle up with **Nigel,** while her father would have to sleep in the dog basket at the end of the bed. The poor man would sneeze all night, as he was allergic to dog hair.

"ACHOO!"

When he woke up in the morning, he was so covered in dog hair he looked like the creature of legend **BIGFOOT.**

BIGFOOT

FATHER

There was one exceedingly unusual thing
about **Nigel.** Something that I'm sure you are
NEVER, EVER going to guess...

This huge beast was absolutely terrified of...

CATS!

"MiAow!"

It is meant to be cats that are terrified of dogs, but
not in this case.

If **Nigel** spotted even a tiny one when out on a walk, he
would shake with fear, and howl like a baby...

"WAHOOO!"

...before leaping up a tree to escape.

WHOOMPH!

The great big scaredy-dog wouldn't then come down
until he was sure the moggy was miles away.

When he did leap to the ground, **Nigel** would flatten poor
Peaches, who would be waiting patiently for
him under the tree.

SPLAT!

The day our story begins, Posy Pooch did the unthinkable.

She got another dog!

Despite **Nigel** being the size of a hundred normal dogs, she decided that the family needed one more. A wife for **Nigel**. Without even telling Peaches or the girl's father, she bought another **Tibetan mastiff**. This one she called *Nigella*.

That afternoon, Dad picked up Peaches from school, and they were coming through the front door when Mum shouted, "SURPRISE!"

"Oh no," muttered Dad, fearing the worst.

"It's not what I think it is, is it?" asked Peaches.

"Well, what do you think it is?" demanded Mum.

"Another dog!" chimed in Dad and Peaches together.

"Well, don't spoil it for yourselves!"

"It is another dog, though, isn't it, Mum?" pressed Peaches.

"Well, you are actually ruining this for me! Just wait!"

Then the lady opened the door to the living room and shouted, "TA-DA!"

There were two of the biggest dogs known to man lying there, taking up the entire room, slobbering all over the carpet.

"What an incredible surprise!" said Peaches sarcastically.

On noticing the little girl and her father, the pair of pooches barked...

"WOOF!"

"RUFF!"

...leaped up and **knocked** them both clean over. Then the mutts **tramped** all over them with their huge paws, before bounding out of the room, nearly knocking the door off its hinges as they went.

"Aren't **Nigel** and *Nigella* absolutely delightful together?" said Mum.

From the floor, Peaches and her father turned to each other and shared a look of horror.

Now you might think things couldn't get any worse. Well, you would be wrong. Because when you have a boy dog and a girl dog, sometimes they have... you guessed it...

PUPPIES!

One night, *Nigella* gave birth to not one, not two, not three, not four— Actually, this is going to take too long. I might as well just tell you how many puppies she had.

Ninety-nine!

Ninety-nine **Tibetan mastiff** puppies in one little house. The puppies might have been smaller than their parents, but by any other standards they were HUGE. Each one was about the size of a Shetland pony.

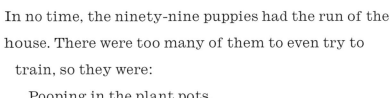

In no time, the ninety-nine puppies had the run of the house. There were too many of them to even try to train, so they were:

Pooping in the plant pots.

POOP!

Climbing on each other's shoulders so they could steal Peaches's sweets from the top shelf of the fridge. SCOFF!

Ripping the girl's schoolbooks to shreds.

RIP!

Chewing everything in sight, including Peaches's toes. GNAW!

Jumping in the pond.

SPLOSH! SPLISH! SPLASH!

Then drying themselves by shaking pond water over the girl.

SHOOK-A-SHOOK-A-SHOOK!

Pee-peeing in Peaches's shoes. PSSSSS! "YUCK!"

Charging up the stairs and knocking Peaches clean over!

STOMP! STOMP! STOMP! WHOOSH!

"ARGH!"

The girl would then tumble down the stairs on her bottom.

BUMP! BUMP! BUMP!

Blowing off right next to her face and then scrambling away at speed.

PFFT! "YUCK!"

Hogging the remote control so Peaches couldn't watch her favourite cartoons on television. Instead, the puppies would only click on dog-themed films. "WOOF!"

As for Peaches, she was forced out of her own bedroom! Her mother had decided that it needed to be a playroom for the puppies.

The girl took to sleeping on the sofa, but would be woken up by a mountain of mutts squatting on her head.

"EURGH! GET OFF!"

As for her father, he'd been moved out of the bedroom entirely, as his wife was now sleeping in the basket.

Posy had given their double bed over to **Nigel** and *Nigella*. Dad had no choice but to sleep in the greenhouse. It wasn't ideal, as the neighbours could see him taking off his pyjamas in the morning. As the old saying goes, people in glass houses... shouldn't undress in daylight.

Finally, Peaches and her father couldn't take any more. One night, they confronted Mum.

"Please, please, please can we give some of the puppies away?" the girl pleaded.

"Away! Why on earth would we give any away?" Mum was shocked.

"Because we have a hundred and one dogs in the house!" exclaimed Dad.

"Well, I have some good news! *Nigella* is expecting again!"

"NOOO!" screamed Peaches and Dad.

"Oh yes! With any luck, there might be another ninety-nine puppies running around here soon!"

"PLEASE, NO!" exploded Dad.

"It's just two hundred dogs. Nothing really. Oh, that reminds me! I will need the greenhouse back soon, and of course the sofa, for the new puppies."

"Where do you want us to sleep, then?" protested Peaches.

Mum thought for a moment. "Both of you could always sleep in the dustbins."

"The dustbins!" Peaches couldn't believe what she was hearing.

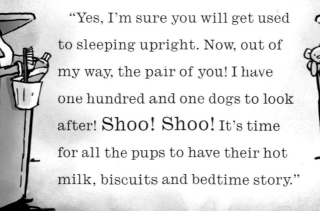

"Yes, I'm sure you will get used to sleeping upright. Now, out of my way, the pair of you! I have one hundred and one dogs to look after! Shoo! Shoo! It's time for all the pups to have their hot milk, biscuits and bedtime story."

Finally, Peaches decided that ENOUGH WAS ENOUGH!

So that night, when it was dark, the girl got up off the sofa and tiptoed out to the greenhouse. There her father was making the best of it by trying to sleep on a bag of compost.

"PSST! DAD!" she hissed, not wanting her mother to know she was conspiring with her father.

"Oh! Hello, love," said Dad, who by now looked completely beaten by life. He was unshaven, unwashed and his hair was sticking up in the most ludicrous way. One side of his face was blackened by compost.

"What are you doing out of bed? I mean off the sofa?" he asked.

"We need to do something about all these dogs! We can't live like this!"

"I know! But what? Soon we are going to be sharing the house with two hundred dogs!"

"I've been thinking, Dad. Nigel is scared of cats, right?"

"Yes! Yes, he is. He runs a mile whenever he sees one."

"Well, maybe Nigella and all the ninety-nine puppies

might be scared of them too. Maybe all **Tibetan mastiffs** are."

"So? We don't have a cat."

"Not yet, but let's buy a kitten!"

"You're a genius!"

Peaches blushed.

First thing in the morning, while Posy was bathing her hundred and one dogs, Peaches and Dad raced to the local pet shop. There they found the most adorable-looking white fluffy kitten, named Snowflake.

When they arrived home, Peaches hid Snowflake under her coat. Once inside the hallway of the house, the girl called out,

"MOTHER!"

"I AM BUSY PREPARING TWO HUNDRED STEAKS FOR THE DOGGIES' BREAKFAST," she hollered from the kitchen at the end of the hallway.

"Oh! Don't worry, Mum. I picked up something I think they'll much prefer," called back Peaches.

"Are you sure about this?" hissed Dad.

"We can always get another kitten!"

"WHAT?" spluttered Dad.

"I am joking, of course! Don't worry. I will keep a firm hold on Snowflake," she replied, taking out the kitten from under her coat and giving the adorable little thing a gentle stroke.

"If you're sure," said Dad.

The girl nodded before shouting, "COME ON, DOGGIES!"

In an instant, one hundred and one dogs were charging towards them.

STOMP! STOMP! STOMP!

Nigel led the pack, with Nigella and the ninety-nine puppies not far behind.

"LOOK, **NIGEL!**" shouted the girl, showing him the kitten.

"MIAOW!" it miaowed.

The sight of the little white fluffy kitten was enough to send a shaking **Nigel** into a fit of howling.

"WOOOOOOOOOH!"

As Peaches had predicted, all the other dogs were scared of the tiny kitten too.

"WOOOOOOOOOOOOOH!"

They all began howling.

"WOOOOOOOOOOOOOOOOOOOOOH!"

"**Hiss!**" hissed Snowflake.

The dogs were terrified. They scrambled over each other as they bounded back down the hallway.

STOMP! STOMP! STOMP!

They flooded into the kitchen. A tsunami of **Tibetan mastiffs**. They swept Mum clean off her feet.

"ARGH!"

She flew into the air.

The dogs charged at the back door, smashing it off its hinges.

BOOM!

Posy Pooch landed on **Nigel's** back.

THOMP!

The dogs scattered into the garden, bursting through the fence...

BASH!

...and disappearing off into the distance.

Mum was still riding on **Nigel's** back, and the dog showed no signs of slowing down.

"HELP!" she cried.

But she was so far away that there was nothing her daughter or husband could do.

Soon the giant dogs were nothing more than dots on the horizon.

"Not sure where they are all off to in such a hurry," remarked Dad.

"By the look of it," began Peaches, "Nigel is running all the way back to Tibet!"

"PURR!" purred the kitten.

TERRY TETCH

N<small>O ONE LIKES QUEUEING.</small> You never meet a single person who says, "My favourite hobby is standing in queues all day long. Then, when I finally get to the front, I go straight to the back so I can queue all over again!"

Queues are boring. Queues are time-consuming.

Queues make your feet ache. But they are a necessity. You have to queue to get to the thing you want to do.

Get on the bus. Have your school dinner. Go on a ride at the fair.

British people are exceptionally good at queueing. Queueing was invented by a British lady, Duchess Queenie Queue, in 1766.

Her husband had just invented the toilet. As it was the only toilet in Britain at that time, there were a lot of people clamouring to use it. Everyone in Britain, in fact. There was nothing short of a stampede of people who needed to go. So the duchess made everyone stand in line to take turns to use her husband's great invention.

The queue for the one and only toilet in the country stretched the entire length of the British Isles. As soon as you had gone, it was sensible to go and join the end of the queue again, as by the time you reached the front you would most likely need to go again.

Now, everyone is expected to queue. However, there once was a man who **refused** to queue. Terry Tetch. If he saw a queue for anything, even a queue of one person (which isn't really a queue until you join it), he would have an **EXTREME REACTION.**

His red hair would stand on END.

His legs would SHAKE.

His glasses would STEAM UP.

His nostrils would FLARE.

And his ears would FLAP so much you might think he was going to TAKE OFF.

Terry always embarrassed his two sons, Ted and Todd, by coming up with the most **extraordinary** excuses for why he should **never** queue.

If there was a long line at their local burger chain, Terry would tell the server,

"I've been lost at sea! I haven't eaten anything for three years except seagull poop. Please, please, I beg you! Let me get my chicken nuggets, chips and chocolate milkshake first!"

Everyone in the line would give the trio dirty looks as Terry dragged the twins to the front.

When there was a crocodile of people waiting to enter the football stadium, Terry would shout,

"I am England's new star striker! I know I am old and a bit podgy, but I am playing today! Let me through!"

Todd and Ted's faces would blush **BRIGHT RED** as their father elbowed his way to the front.

Worst of all was when Terry was faced with a really **long** queue to get on the bus.

"Let me through!" he shouted, pulling the twins along, and barging people out of the way. "This bus isn't going anywhere without me!"

"How is that so?" called out an elderly lady struggling with her shopping trolley.

"Because I have to sit at the back and pedal!"

Todd and Ted wished the ground would swallow them up!

The twin brothers were turning ten, so their father asked them what they would like to do as a special birthday treat.

"I promise to take you **anywhere** you like!" he said. "Just name it! Anywhere at all!"

The twins looked at each other, and then both said in unison…

"Loopyland!"

"NOOOOOOO!" cried Dad.

Wilt Loopy was an American billionaire who made cartoon films and who had built the world's greatest theme park. He'd died as an old man many years ago, but he'd had his head deep-frozen, so he could be brought back to life in the future. Now the future had arrived, and his head was attached to a robot body, and he was back running his *Loopy* empire.

Wilt Loopy's most famous character was *Loopy* the Leopard, a leopard who was – you guessed it – loopy. The character had been around for nearly a hundred years, and could be found on children's lunchboxes, pencil cases and underpants, often hollering his catchphrase...

"LOOPY! LOOPY! LOO!"

So loved were all things *Loopy* that children from all over the world dreamed of one day going to *Loopyland.*

The only problem with *Loopyland* was the queues.

The queues for the most popular rides were so long that they snaked for miles around the park. You could spend the entire day queueing for the *Loop-the-loop* Loopycoaster, or the *Loopy* Logflume, or Little *Loopyland,* and then the ride would be over in a matter of moments. The *Loopy* Haunted House attraction lasted just one second. You walked in the front door, a teenager in a *Loopy* the Leopard costume shouted, "BOO!" at you, and then shoved you out through the back door.

There was nowhere on earth that Terry Tetch would rather NOT be than *Loopyland. Loopyland* was a NIGHTMARE for someone who hated queues, but but but...! He had promised his boys.

So, how could Terry take his twins to *Loopyland* and not have to queue?

The man needed a plan.

Terry's great-great-great-aunt
lived in the attic of the family home.
AUNT URSULA was a terrifying snake of a lady,
forever hissing and baring her **FALSE FANGS** if the boys
came too near. She was absolutely ancient –
no one knew how old exactly, not even her.
AUNT URSULA had a metal frame called a
walker, in case she ever went out, but she
never did, preferring to bark orders at
the Tetch family to do her bidding.

Terry had a naughty idea. If only he could "borrow" the walker for the trip to *Loopyland,* then he could pretend he couldn't stand well enough to wait in line. The staff at *Loopyland* would let him go straight to the front of the queue for every single ride!

The plan was so simple it was brilliant.

There was one big problem: how would Terry get his hands on his great-great-great-aunt's walker?

There was no way the old snake would let him have it. Even though she lived in the attic of his home, she loathed her great-great-great-nephew.

Terry decided a dawn raid was the best plan. So, on the day of the trip to *Loopyland,* Terry crept upstairs to the attic and, without a sound, opened the door. "ZZZ! ZZZZ! ZZZZZ!" AUNT URSULA was snoring away. Her false teeth or, rather, fangs were sunk in a glass of water on her bedside table, and her walker squatted next to it. Terry tiptoed over to the walker, picked it up and swung it over the bed. As he did so, one of the walker's four metal legs clunked into the glass of water containing the old snake's FALSE FANGS.

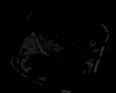

NOOO! thought Terry as
the glass, water and **FALSE FANGS** hit the floor.
TINK! SPLOSH! DOOF!
The fangs clattered across the floorboards as if they
were alive!

CLATTER!

CLATTER!

CLATTER!

The noise woke up **AUNT URSULA** with a start. She opened one **beady** eye. Then another.

"WHAT ARE YOU DOING WITH MY WALKER, YOU NASTY LITTLE SQUIRT?" she bawled, though her words sounded a bit muffled as she didn't have her **FALSE FANGS** in.

"Erm, just borrowing it, **AUNT URSULA**!" Terry replied, dashing to the door with the walker.

Stupidly, he was holding the walker widthways, so it smashed into the doorframe.

TWuNK!

It allowed just enough time for the old snake to slide out of bed and on to the floor.

SLUMP!

Then she scooped up her escaping **FALSE FANGS** with her long, bony fingers, and pushed them into her mouth.

"SSSSSSSSS!" she hissed.

Next she slithered across the floor on her tummy, and dug her fangs into her great-great-great-nephew's ankle.

CHOMP!

"AARRGGHH!" screamed Terry.

He speedily spun the walker round, and charged down the stairs.

STOMP! STOMP! STOMP!

AUNT URSULA was still biting his ankle! And she was NOT letting go. She slid down the staircase behind him...

SLUNK! SLUNK! SLUNK!

...all the time sinking her fangs deeper and deeper into Terry's flesh.

"AAARRRGGGHHH!"

On hearing their father scream, Ted and Todd leaped up out of their bunk beds.

"D-A-D?" yelled Ted.

"WHAT'S GOING ON?" shouted Todd.

"GET IN THE CAR!" ordered their father.

"BUT," they replied, "WE ARE STILL IN OUR PYJAMAS!"

"I SAID, 'GET IN THE CAR!'"

The boys did as they were told.

125

They hurtled down the stairs, hurried out of the front door and bundled themselves into the back of the car. Meanwhile, **AUNT URSULA** was slowing Terry down to a stop. As much as he tried to shake her off, the old snake just wouldn't let go.

There was only one thing for it. Terry leaned down, and tickled his great-great-great-aunt under her chin.

She half laughed, half screamed, opening her mouth...

"HAAAAAAAH!"

...leaving her **FANGS** still biting into his ankle!

Terry made a dash for it, slamming the front door behind him.

SHUNT!

Still holding the walker, he tried to force it into the car through the door, but it was too wide and just wouldn't go.

KERPLUNK! KERCHUNK! KERNUNK!

Thinking fast, he whipped the belt off his dressing gown, and lashed the walker to the roof of the car. Then he leaped into the driver's seat, and started the engine.

When the plane (with the walker strapped to its roof) finally landed in America, Terry stopped off at the first shop at the airport. There he bought a tin of **talcum powder** and a black pen.

"What do you need those for, Dad?" asked Ted, still in his pyjamas.

"Just you watch!" he replied.

Then he proceeded to tip the whole tin of **talcum powder** over his **head**.

WOOMPH!

A huge white cloud exploded into the airport, which made the boys cough and splutter.

"What on earth are you doing?" demanded Todd, also still in his pyjamas.

"I haven't finished yet!" replied Terry, proceeding to draw lines on his face with the pen.

"Have you gone nuts, Dad?" asked Ted, not unreasonably.

"FAR FROM IT!" replied the man with a mischievous grin. "And don't call me 'Dad' any more – call me 'Granddad'! In fact, don't call me 'Granddad' – call me 'Great-Granddad'! Watch!"

With that, Dad grabbed the walker and shuffled along the airport walkway.

SHIFFLE! SHUFFLE! SHAFFLE!

He was pretending to be a very, very, very old man, complete with white hair and thick lines all over his face.

BEFORE

AFTER

"This way we won't have to queue for a single ride at *Loopyland!*"

"But we don't mind queueing, do we, Todd?" asked Ted.

"No. Everyone else has to, so why shouldn't we?" agreed Todd.

"BECAUSE I CANNOT QUEUE!" yelled Terry Tetch.

He was so loud that everyone in the airport looked round. Realising his mistake, Terry instantly went back to being the boys' great-grandfather and shuffled off towards the exit.

SHIFFLE! SHUFFLE! SHAFFLE!

"I've got a **bad** feeling about this!" remarked Ted.

"Me too!" added Todd.

A short while later, the three found themselves outside the tall gates to the world's greatest theme park.

Loopyland!

Ted and Todd could barely contain their excitement. The boys were literally jumping up and down with joy.

BOING! BOING! BOI

Of course, their father was doing no such thing. Instead, he was holding tightly to the walker, and shuffling slowly towards the ticket office, past the mile-long line of folks queueing to buy their tickets.

"H-h-hello!" began Terry, even putting on an old **wobbly** voice to go with his supposedly old **wobbly** legs. "P-p-please can you help me?" he asked the ticket-seller. "I am one hundred and one years old."

"So?" asked the bored bubble-gum-blowing teenager behind the window.

"So, I am very old, and don't w-w-walk too good – that's why I have got this old thing!" he said, rattling his walker.

RITTLE! RUTTLE! RATTLE!

"And, young man, I definitely, one hundred per cent, without any doubt whatsoever, cannot queue. Not even for a second! Do you hear me? NOT ONE SECOND!"

The ticket-seller rolled his eyes, and reached for a metal box.

"Here you go, Grandpa!" he said as he slid three GOLD PASSES under the window.

"YES! NO QUEUEING!" exclaimed Terry, jumping up and down.

As he did so, a fog of **talcum powder** clouded the air.

"What's that?"

asked the ticket-seller.

"Erm, it's, well..." he spluttered.

Dad was in

TROUBLE.

The impossibly long queue of folks waiting began eyeballing him suspiciously.

"DANDRUFF!" cried Terry, thinking fast.

"That's a heck of a lot of dandruff! Welcome to *Loopyland!*" said the ticket-seller. "NEXT!"

GOLD PASSES meant they could go straight to the front of *any* queue in the whole of *Loopyland*.

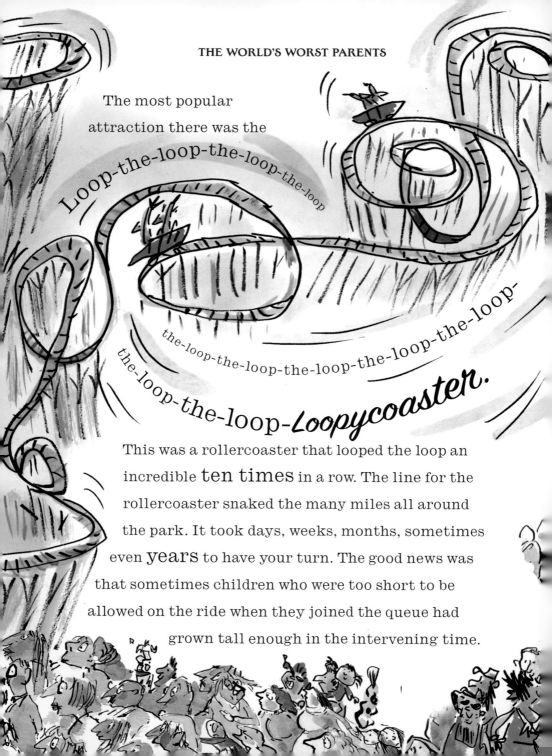

The most popular attraction there was the Loop-the-loop-the-loop-the-loop the-loop-the-loop-the-loop-the-loop-the-loop the-loop-the-loop-*Loopycoaster.*

This was a rollercoaster that looped the loop an incredible **ten times** in a row. The line for the rollercoaster snaked the many miles all around the park. It took days, weeks, months, sometimes even **years** to have your turn. The good news was that sometimes children who were too short to be allowed on the ride when they joined the queue had grown tall enough in the intervening time.

So, after a huge lunch of *Loopyburger*, *Loopyfries* and *Loopychocoshake*, the Tetch family made their way to the rollercoaster.

"I'm not sure about this," hissed Ted.

"It's the longest line I've ever seen!" added Todd. "People are going to hate us, Dad!"

"SHUSH!" shushed their father. "It's Great-Grandfather, remember! Trust me. We will go straight to the front!"

The two boys shook their heads as they followed their father to the front of the queue, Terry shuffling on AUNT URSULA's walker all the way.

SHIFFLE! SHUFFLE! SHAFFLE!

The old snake's FALSE FANGS were still locked on to his ankle.

Those families who had been waiting to ride the rollercoaster for an eternity, some holding babies that had been born during the time their parents had been queueing, fumed at seeing the three push past them.

"HEY!"   "WHO DO YOU THINK YOU ARE?"

"GET TO THE BACK OF THE LINE!"

"C-c-come along, my g-g-great-g-g-grandsons!" called Terry in his best **wobbly** voice.

Ted and Todd looked at each other nervously and walked through the gates to the ride. Instantly, they were seated in the front row of the *Loopycoaster.* Terry had the smuggest of smug grins on his face as the carriages **chugged** up the impossibly steep slope that seemed to stretch all the way to the sky.

This was the calm before the storm.

The storm came.

As soon as the peak had been reached, the carriages careered down at terrific speed.

ZOOM!

They looped the first loop. Ted and Todd noticed that their father's face was beginning to turn green. That *Loopyburger,* those *Loopyfries* and that *Loopychocoshake* were coming back for an encore.

LOOP!

As each loop passed, Terry Tetch's face became greener and greener.

TERRY TETCH

LOOP!

At first it was a light green.

LOOP!

Then a dark green.

LOOP!

Before becoming a parrot green.

The next thing they knew, their father's face had turned a putrid green. *LOOP!*

No! A luminous green!

LOOP!

A DAYGLO GREEN!

LOOP!

A FLUORESCENT GREEN!

LOOP!

Before settling on a VOMIT GREEN!

This meant only one thing.

Their father was about to spew.

SPLURGE!

And spew he did. Because of the G-force of travelling so fast upside down, the **CHUNDER THUNDER** came out of his mouth...

HURL!

...and splurged right back in his face.

SPLAT!

As the final loop was looped, Terry Tetch found himself covered from head to toe in his own **YACK ATTACK.**

At last the rollercoaster came to an abrupt halt.

S C H T U M !

Ted and Todd helped their poor father off the ride. The man couldn't see a thing, and rubbed his head with his sleeve.

WIPE!

At once, the old-age lines from the pen came off, as did, of course, all that talcum powder with which he'd covered his hair.

The hundred-and-one-year-old man had been unmasked in front of the entire queue for the *Loopycoaster.*

"HE'S A FAKER!"

"HE'S NO OLD DUDE!"

"HE JUMPED THE QUEUE!"

The angry shouts came thick and fast.

"I, er, um, I am a g-g-great-g-g-grandpa!" protested Terry.

"LIAR!"

"CHEAT!"

"PHONY!"

Looking at the angry mob circling, Terry shouted,

"RUN!"

Run he did, his boys trailing close behind.

There was no time to grab **AUNT URSULA**'s walker, which was left discarded by the side of the rollercoaster.

"HE NEVER EVEN NEEDED THAT THING!"

"WHAT A PIECE OF WORK!"

"GET HIM!"

In no time, the entire queue of people for the *Loopycoaster* was chasing the Tetch family.

The three ran straight into a huge *Loopyland* musical parade.

The great Wilt Loopy himself was at the front, his old head on his new robot body, with all his cartoon animal chums following on behind, singing the *Loopyland* song.

"WE LOVE *Loopyland!*
Loopyland WE LOVE!
IF YOU DON'T LOVE *Loopyland,*
OFF YOU CAN SHOVE!"

There was *Loopy* the Leopard, of course.

BARMY the Baboon.   **WACKY** the Walrus.

Nutty the Newt.   **Crackers** the Crocodile.

And **WOMBA** the Wombat.

As Terry Tetch barged through the parade, he did the unthinkable. He knocked over Wilt Loopy!

THUD!

"Argh!" yelped the billionaire as his old head became detached from his new robot body, and rolled off.

TRUNDLE!

As Terry and his sons raced away, the detached head shouted,

"Cartoon animals of *Loopyland!* After them!"

"DAD! I CAN'T RUN ANY MORE! I'VE GOT A STITCH!" called Ted, clutching his tummy.

"AND I'VE GOT WOBBLY WOBBLY LEGS!" complained Todd.

Ahead was a *Loopyland Loopymobile.* Terry pulled the driver out and jumped in.

"COME ON, BOYS!" he shouted, and Ted and Todd leaped in the back. As the *Loopymobile* raced off, the cartoon animals caught up and pounced on it.

Loopy the Leopard was on the bonnet.

BARMY the Baboon was on the roof.

WACKY the Walrus was on the windscreen.

Nutty the Newt was on the boot.

Crackers the Crocodile was clinging on to the door.

And **WOMBA** the Wombat was on the back window.

Terry drove the *Loopymobile* as fast as he could, swerving into ice-cream vans and toy stands to try to shake them off.

CRASH!

BANG!

WALLOP!

One by one, the animals were hurled to the ground.

Only *Loopy* the Leopard remained. The cartoon animal crawled around into the footwell of the buggy.

"GET OFF!" shouted Terry.

But *Loopy* the Leopard went to grab the man's ankle to stop him pushing down on the accelerator pedal. As he did so, *Loopy* pressed hard on **AUNT URSULA**'s **FALSE FANGS** that were still locked on to Terry's flesh!

"OOOOOOOoooooWWWWWWWWWWEEEEEEEEEE!"

screamed Terry. His foot came off the accelerator pedal, and the *Loopymobile* lurched to a halt.

Ted turned to Todd. "We are in big trouble."

"The biggest," replied Todd to Ted.

WOMBA the Wombat had picked up Wilt Loopy's head, and brought it over to them. The old man had gone scarlet with fury. "Think you don't need to queue, do you? I am going to teach you a lesson you will never forget!"

The cartoon animals grabbed the Tetch family and

marched them through *Loopyland* as the crowds of visitors all jeered.

"BOOO!"

"*Loopyland* fans," called out Wilt Loopy's detached head, "I need your help! I need you all to form the longest queue you can for the

Loop-the-loop-the-loop-the-loop-the-loop-the-loop-the-loop-the-loop-the-loop-the-loop-the-loop-the-loop-the-loop-the-loop-the-loop-Loopycoaster.

There's a *Loopyland* pencil for everyone who does! Completely free!"

Instantly, everyone did what the kindly billionaire's head asked.

"Thanks a billion!" said the head. "Now take this man to the back of it!"

Terry was sweating and shaking as the cartoon animals dragged him to the back of the queue. As he was placed there, his hair stood up on end, his glasses steamed up, his nostrils flared, his legs shook and his ears flapped so much he actually lifted off the ground.

WHOOSH!

Terry was shaking so much that the old snake's **FALSE FANGS** fell off his ankle.

CLATTER!

"Whose are these?" asked Wilt Loopy's head.

"My great-great-great-**AUNT URSULA**'s," replied Terry.

"Well, the poor old dear must be needing them back! I bet she is a kindly soul. Pick them up, please, somebody. I would, but I have no hands, arms or, indeed, body. I will call this **AUNT URSULA**, such a *pretty* name, and reunite her with her teeth. Now, your boys have done nothing wrong. Their only crime is having a terrible father. Boys, you can have a free *Loopynugget.*"

Ted and Todd smiled. "Thank you."

"Just one *Loopynugget* to share," continued Wilt Loopy's head, before returning his gaze to Terry. "YOU! You will be made to stand and wait. For the longest time anyone has ever waited for anything!"

So Terry waited. And waited. And waited.

His ears flapped so much that he had to be tied to the ground to stop him from flying off.

His glasses cracked.

FLAP!
FLAP!
FLAP!

And then he waited some **more.**

His hair stood on end.

What seemed like a lifetime passed before Terry was finally at the front of the queue, and ready to take his seat on the *Loopycoaster.*

The safety bar came down, pinning him to his seat, and the *Loopycoaster* began its slow ascent to the sky. Terry turned his head to see who was sitting next to him.

147

HORROR UPON HORROR!
It was **AUNT URSULA!**

The old snake turned to him, opened her mouth and bared her **FANGS**.

"REVENGE!" she **hissed** as she leaned over to take a bite.

"NOOO!" screamed Terry.

"NOOOOOOOOOOOOOOOOOOOO!"

MISS TUTELAGE

The mother who was
also her son's teacher

BOOKS

BOOKS

AND MORE BOOKS

MISS
TUTELAGE

HORROR UPON HORROR upon horror. Just imagine if your mum was also... your teacher. It is the WORST of both worlds!

Think: you are in your room, lying on your bed, listening to some music, when your mum/teacher bursts in and demands, "SPELL 'EMBARRASSMENT'!"

Or, even worse, you are at school in the middle of a Maths lesson when your mum/teacher bursts in and says, "Can I have your dirty socks and underpants now? I am nipping home to put on a boil wash!"

And the entire classroom of thirty children laugh their heads off.

"HA! HA! HA!"

This is exactly the nightmare that Thomas Tutelage was facing when moving up from little school to big school. His mother, Tudor Tutelage, was an English teacher at **WHOPPING HIGH**, the school where Thomas was about to become one of her pupils.

The pair lived together in a tiny house bursting with books. There were books on shelves, piled up on the floor and stacked on tables. They were Miss Tutelage's passion, and one she shared with her son. Thomas was something of a swot, and always had his nose in a book.

His mother was an old-fashioned lady, who wore thick glasses and had an explosion of **Frizzy** hair. The first thing anyone noticed about her, though, was her height, or, rather, lack of it. Miss Tutelage only came up to most people's waists.

Thomas had inherited the same explosion of **Frizzy** hair, the need to wear thick glasses and the lack of height from his mother. Of course, the boy loved his mum, but he did find her **embarrassing** at times.

She was the kind of mother who, when you were out at the shops, would ask every ten seconds if you needed a pee. Or say in front of your friends, "Now, son, did you remember to wipe your botty?"

So it will come as no surprise to you that Thomas had grave misgivings about becoming a pupil at his mother's school.

The night before his first day, the boy sat up in his bed and asked, "Mum, what's it going to be like tomorrow? Us both being at the same school and all that?"

"Oh, **Tiny Tom-Tom...!**" she began, putting down her son's hot milk and perching on the edge of his bed.

The boy grimaced. How he hated being called **Tiny Tom-Tom!**

"It will be *magically wondrous* and *wondrously magical*," continued Mother. "Just think, first thing tomorrow morning, we'll be sitting side by side on the school bus like two peas in a pod! Together we can recite all the times tables to pass the time! Or, even better, sing the Alphabet Song! **A, B, C...!** What larks!"

NO! thought Thomas. He wanted to be laughing

and joking with the other kids on the school bus, not doing the two-times table and singing his way through all the letters of the alphabet!

"Then Mummy can take the register!" she continued. "I've made sure you are in my class! And I won't need to call out your name, **Tom-Tom** – I can just say, 'Darling, are you here?' and you can reply, 'Here, Mummy dearest!'"

NOO! thought Thomas. This was getting worse and worse.

"Then we can share refreshing squash and yummy scrummy biscuits at breaktime! Fiddle-dee-dee!"

NOOO! Nothing fiddle-dee-dee or indeed fiddle-dum-dum about it!

"Now I know what you're thinking – I will be missing my mummy until lunchtime!"

I WILL NOT BE THINKING THAT! he thought. *NOT IN A BILLION YEARS!*

"We won't be missing each other too much, because we will have our lessons together, silly-billy bumkins!"

NOOOO! DON'T CALL ME SILLY-BILLY BUMKINS!

"And I know you will always be tip-top of the class, as you will have extra lessons at home!"

NOOOOO! The boy wanted to spend his weekends playing footy in the park, not inside doing extra lessons!

"All the other boys and girls will think you are so cool coming top of the class every single time!"

NOOOOOOO, THEY WON'T! IT WILL REALLY ANNOY THEM!

"And then, instead of having lunch in the noisy old dining hall, me and you can have our own delightful little picnic on the lawn outside! Just the two of us!"

NOOOOOOOO!

"You won't be missing your friends, because any time you like we can give them a little wave together: 'Woo-hoo!'"

NOOOOOOOOOO! NO ONE IS EVER GOING 'Woo-hoo!' TO ANYONE!

"Then after school Mummy will have to take detention, so instead of going home and watching cartoons you can sit in on detention with me! It's only an hour or two, and you can get on with your homework or, if you fancy, you can write some lines yourself! Lines can be fun, fun, fun! Don't worry, I will tell the naughty children that you haven't done anything bad and are, in fact, the bestest boy in the whole of WHOPPING HIGH , if not the world!"

NOOOOOOOOOOOO! THIS SOUNDS LIKE THE WORST DAY EVER!

"So, how does all that sound, **Tiny Tom-Tom?** Pretty perfect, if you ask me!"

Perfectly awful, more like, thought the boy. Thomas didn't know where to start. It was all toe-curlingly, tummy-turningly, buttock-clenchingly HIDEOUS! None of what his mother said could ever happen, or his life would be OVER. Thomas would be a laughing stock, not just with the kids but with the teachers too.

A laughing stock for **ever** and **ever** and **ever** and then for some more on top.

"HA! HA! HA! HA! HA! HA! HA! HA! HA! HA! HA! HA! HA! HA! HA! HA! HA! HA!"

"Mum?" began Thomas hesitantly. He was a nice boy and didn't want to be cruel. He had to choose his words carefully.

"Yes, **Tom-Tom?**" she replied brightly.

"Don't take this the wrong way, but..."

"But?"

"But when I go to WHOPPING HIGH , can we please pretend we **aren't** related?"

Silence.

Mother's eyes welled with tears, and a look of terrible sadness settled on her face.

"You are joking, **Tom-Tom?**"

"No, I am not joking, Mother!"

"B-b-but why on earth would we pretend not to know

each other, **Tom-Tom?**" she stammered. "There is no greater bond than that special bond between mother and son."

Thomas sighed. He didn't want to say it, but he had to. "Because if everyone knows you are my mum it is going to be REALLY embarrassing!"

Silence again.

"But why? **Tom-Tom,** you are not ashamed of your dear old mother, are you?" she pleaded.

"No!" he replied, a little too quickly to be believed. "It's just..."

"Just what?" she pressed.

"Just it will be better this way. This way I can just blend in with all the other kids. And don't worry. We don't have to pretend not to know each other for long. It's only for the next seven years!"

His mother's eyes blossomed with tears. "I just have some marking to do!" she lied as she fled from her son's bedroom.

"Oops!" said the boy. His hot milk was now cold milk, so he lay down to sleep.

*

Dawn broke on Thomas's first day at **WHOPPING HIGH**. After a frosty breakfast,* mother and son walked to the bus stop without a word. Then when the school bus came the pair sat at different ends, Mother at the very front and Thomas at the very back.

An older girl with sticky-out ears sat down next to a nervous-looking Thomas. The boy's eyes were darting around the bus, checking no one was staring at him. The girl, Clodagh, leaned closer and peered at him.

"New boy, are you?" she asked.

"Me? Yes."

"Do you know, you look exactly like Miss Tutelage," she observed.

"Who is she?" asked the boy, mock innocently.

"The English teacher! She is sitting right there!" said Clodagh, pointing to the front of the school bus.

Thomas looked at the lady. "I have never seen her before in my life!" he replied.

---

* I mean they ate in chilly silence, not that they had Frosties. They actually had cornflakes.

Clodagh was not convinced. "Same hair. Same thick glasses. Same problem reaching for things on high shelves. I would bet a year's pocket money she's your **mother!**"

"**No!**" he snapped. "She's not! I don't know that woman at all. Now please let me get on with some private reading!" He then brought out the complete works of *William Shakespeare* from his satchel and began to flick through the pages.

Clodagh smiled to herself. She knew the boy was hiding something.

Thomas sighed with relief when the bus ride came to an end. Still not looking at each other, mother and son passed through the school gates. A tall sign outside read WHOPPING HIGH . Thomas was immediately struck by how much the other children towered over him. Some of the bigger boys even had moustaches. Not **bushy ones** or fluffy ones, but moustaches all the same.

Miss Tutelage peeled off towards her classroom, while Thomas Tutelage peeled off towards his. The boy looked to check his mother had kept going, when...

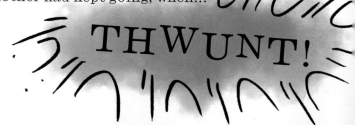
THWUNT!

Thomas Tutelage bounded into the two **biggest boys** in school.

TROUBLE!

These two didn't just have moustaches – they had fluff all over their faces. Bearded boys! If you could call these brutes boys… They were men, really. They must have been eighteen years old, even though they looked older. Maybe they'd been kept down a school year every year for about twenty years for failing all their exams. Whatever – they were definitely the **biggest** boys in the school, and Thomas Tutelage was the littlest.

The pair were actually identical twins.

DOUBLE TROUBLE!

Ray and Roy Slab.

"Sorry!" chirped Thomas, hoping that would be the end of it. Sadly, that was only the start of it.

"WOT YOU LOOKING AT?" one of them barked.

It was Ray.

Anyone who has ever been asked this question by a bully will know that there is no good answer. Whatever you say, there will be trouble.

TRIPLE TROUBLE!

"Your knee," replied Thomas. It was a perfectly reasonable reply, as he was indeed head height with this monster's knobbly knee.

"ARE YOU TRYING TO BE FUNNY?" barked the other. That was Roy.

Now, anyone who has been asked this question by a bully will know that, once again, any answer you give is going to make things worse.

YES – you get a **thump.**

NO – you also get a **thump.**

"Not sure," spluttered the boy.

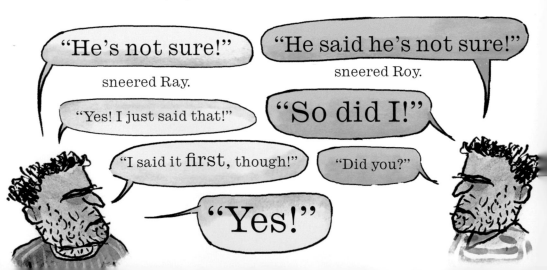

"He's not sure!" sneered Ray.

"He said he's not sure!" sneered Roy.

"Yes! I just said that!"

"So did I!"

"I said it first, though!"

"Did you?"

"Yes!"

The being-kept-back-a-year-every-year-for-twenty-years thing seemed increasingly likely. Ray and Roy were not destined to solve the world's energy crisis any time soon. As they argued between themselves, Thomas began to tiptoe off to his classroom.

"WHERE DO YOU THINK YOU'RE GOING?" demanded Ray.

Once again, there was no answer that could make things better.

"Sneaky little runt!" growled Roy. "He looks like that English teacher, Miss... er... Tutti-Frutti, no, I mean Miss... um... Tutankhamun, Miss... erm... Archbishop Desmond Tutu!"

"No, I don't look like Miss Tutelage, if that is who you mean!" protested Thomas.

"Oh! Aren't you a **clever clogs**, being able to pronounce Tuta... Tuty... Tuto..."

The brute still couldn't pronounce it.

"We need to teach the sneaky little swot a lesson!" said Ray.

With that, the terrible twins began bearing down on the boy.

By now a crowd was forming a circle round them in the playground.

"He's taken on the Slab twins!" shouted a dark-haired boy named Michael.

"On his first day at school!" cried out the spotty girl standing near him.

"He's BANANAS!" concluded a boy with a broken nose.

"LET'S PLAY BASKETBALL WITH HIM!" said Roy.

"I-I-I'm t-t-too short t-t-to p-p-play b-b-basket-b-b-ball!" stammered Thomas.

"You don't need to be tall! You are going to be the ball!" said Ray, picking the boy up by his collar, before scrunching him up into the shape of a ball.

Then Ray tossed him to Roy.

WHOOSH! went Thomas through the air.

"HELP!" called out the boy. "You can't get away with this!"

"Oh, we can get away with anything!" said Roy, catching him and hurling him back.

WHOOSH!

"HOW?"

demanded a flying
Thomas.
"OUR DAD, MR SLAB,
TEACHES HERE!"
It was difficult to imagine things
getting worse, but worse things
got. Instead of tossing the boy across
the playground, the Slab twins now began
bouncing him up and down on his bottom.

BOING! **BOING!** **BOING!**
The bullies dribbled and passed
the boyball or ballboy all the way
along to the hoop at the end of the
playground. Before he knew it,
Thomas was lobbed high
into the air...
WHOOSH!

...and landed in the hoop.

TWANG!

Despite being small for his age, Thomas was bigger than a basketball, and had become stuck in the hoop.

"HELP!" he cried. "SOMEBODY GET A TEACHER!"

"WE'LL GET A TEACHER, YOU LITTLE SNITCH!" snapped Roy, and in no time their father had appeared.

"BOO!" booed the children in the playground as Mr Slab appeared from round the corner of the sports hall. They all loathed the great big brutish bully. He made them do cross-country runs in rain, wind and snow.

"OH, SHUT UP! THE LOT OF YOU!" he barked back.

Mr Slab was even taller than his sons. The beast was bulging out of his bright-red tracksuit and had a thick black beard that went all the way down to his belly button, which was on display. His eyebrows were like two big furry caterpillars, and hair sprouted from every place imaginable. His ears. His nose. His ankles. His neck. Even the palms of his hands were hairy, and that isn't even true of an orang-utan.*

SPOT THE DIFFERENCE

MR SLAB'S HAND

ORANG-UTAN'S HAND

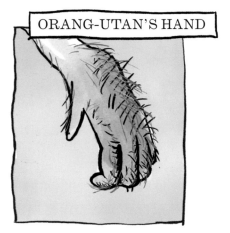

"What's going on here, then?" muttered Slab Senior. He was so tall he was able to reach up to the hoop and pluck the boy out by his collar.

"Thank you, Mr Slab!" exclaimed Thomas.

If the boy thought the teacher had come to rescue him, he was wrong.

"Oh! Got your ball stuck, did you, boys?" the man chuckled.

* **WALLYFACT:** The word "orang-utan" means "great, big, long-haired orange ape thingummy" in Latin.

"Yeah, Dad!" snorted his sons.

"Here you go!" he said, before hurling the boy back to his twins.

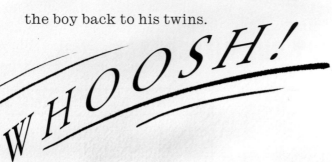

W H O O S H!

"ARGH!" screamed Thomas.

"For goodness' sake, call for your mum, Miss Tutelage!" cried out Clodagh, the girl from the bus. She had rushed into the playground with the growing hordes of children.

"For the last time, Miss Tutelage is not my mother!" called the boy.

"What is the matter with you?" huffed Clodagh, steam coming from her sticky-out ears. She darted out of the playground as the boy was hurled from one Slab to another.

Some of the children tried to help Thomas by jumping up on the three monsters.

But none could match the **might** of the Slabs, and they were hurled to the ground.

Thomas closed his eyes. He couldn't take any more. What he didn't see was his mother charging out of the school building, pulling a trolley full of books, with Clodagh trailing behind.

"I WAS RIGHT!" exclaimed the girl.

"Yes! She's my mother! And, Mother, I am sorry but I really need you to save me right now!"

"CLEAR OFF, FOUR-EYES!" shouted Mr Slab at Miss Tutelage. "WE'RE HAVING FUN!"

The worried mother watched as her son sailed past her through the sky.

"RIGHT! YOU ASKED FOR IT!" she declared. She turned to the girl. "Clodagh, Austen, please!"

"*Pride and Prejudice*?"

"No! *The Complete Works*, please!"

Clodagh ran her eyes along the long line of books until she found the hefty tome.

"THE COMPLETE WORKS OF MISS JANE AUSTEN!"

she chirped.

"Thank you kindly, Clodagh! GOLD STAR!" said Miss Tutelage.

"Thank you, miss!"

Then the teacher marched over to Ray and thwacked him so hard with the book...

THWUCK!

...that he flew all the way over the fence...

WHOOSH!

"ARGH!"

...and landed headfirst in a pond.

SPLOSH!

Ray's big fat feet could be seen poking out of the water as ducks pecked at his bottom.

All the kids in the playground cheered to see this bully finally get his comeuppance.

"HURRAH!"

"One down, two to go," muttered the lady. "Wilde, I think, next!"

"Yes, miss!" said Clodagh, and in an instant she found the right book. One of her favourites.

"THE PLAYS AND POEMS OF MR OSCAR WILDE." "Another GOLD STAR, Clodagh!" said the teacher, taking the weighty volume.

"Thank you, miss!"

Brandishing the book, Miss Tutelage charged at Roy, who was in the middle of hurling her son back to his dad.

THWU**C**K!

She thwacked Roy so wildly with Wilde that he shot up into the air...

W**H**OO**S**H!

"NOOOOOO!"

...before coming back down and landing on a very tall tree. Roy hit every branch on the way down...

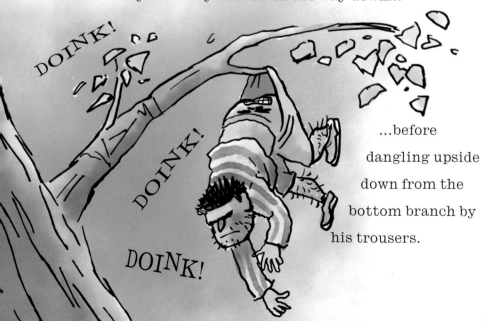

DOINK!

DOINK!

DOINK!

...before dangling upside down from the bottom branch by his trousers.

Everyone could see Roy's bright-green Incredible Hulk underpants!

"ARGH!"

Once again, all the kids roared their approval.

"HURRAH!"

This left only one Slab standing. Mr Slab.

"You wouldn't dare, Frizzball!" he exclaimed.

"Oh, I do dare, Mr Slab, I do dare. Now, let me think… DICKENS!"

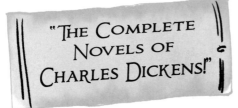 announced Clodagh as she strained to lift the leather-bound book, the heftiest of the lot.

"I can't lift it, miss! I am sorry!" she cried. "Charles Dickens wrote a lot of novels."

"Fifteen novels! But we can do it together, Clodagh!" Miss Tutelage chirped, and together they charged at Mr Slab with the book.

"I WILL THROW YOUR SON!" he threatened.

"CAREFUL, MOTHER!" shouted Thomas.

"KIDS!" she called out to the children in the playground.

"YES?" they called back.

"GET READY TO CATCH MY **TOM-TOM!**"

"WHAT THE—?" began Thomas.

But before he could say whatever he was going to say next his mother and her **STAR** pupil charged at the PE teacher.

Mr Slab threw the boy high into the air.

"NOOO!" cried Thomas as he flew upwards.

WHOOSH!

Just then...

THWUCK!

Mr Slab was hit by fifteen Dickens novels all at once, and he shot up into the air.

"AAARRRGGGHHH!!!" he screamed.

WHOOSH!

Travelling up through the sky, Mr Slab met Thomas on his way down.

WHOOSH!

"Bad luck, sir!" said the boy as he landed on a sea of little arms.

Slab could feel himself slowing. He lingered in the air for a moment, before beginning

his descent.

"CATCH ME!" he called out to the kids below, but they all scattered out of the way and he landed in a dustbin.

CLANK!

"Best place for him!" remarked Miss Tutelage as the kids in the playground celebrated.

"HURRAH!"

Thomas ran into his mother's arms, and she scooped him up.

"Thank you, Mother dearest!" he said.

"Oh!" smarted the lady. "I thought you were embarrassed by me!"

"I'm sorry. No. You are the **best, bravest mother** in the whole wide world, and I love you!"

Right in front of everyone, he gave
his mum a great big kiss.

MWAH!

*"And I love you too, my precious,
adorable, delightful Tiny Tom-Tom."*

"I can see why he pretended not to
know her," muttered Clodagh.

BRRIING!

The bell rang for the start of
lessons.

"Well, what an eventful first
day!" remarked Miss Tutelage.

"It certainly has been," replied
her son.

"Now, after all that excitement, **Tom-Tom,**" she said, "are
you sure you don't need a poo-poo?"

"MOTHER!" cried the boy, before they both burst
out laughing.

"HA! HA! HA!"

All the other children laughed too.

"HA! HA! HA!"

Even though his mother taught at the school, Thomas was never, ever bullied or teased again. That's because everyone now knew that Miss Tudor Tutelage was

ONE MEAN MOMMA!

MONTY MONOPOLIZE

The father who kept his
boys' toys all for himself

MINE

MINE

MINE

MONTY MONOPOLIZE

ONCE THERE WERE two brothers who **dreaded** their birthdays, Christmas time and even Easter. Surely all children love receiving presents?

No. Not these two.

Moe and Curly loathed those times of the year. The

reason was simple. Their father, Monty Monopolize, would give the boys toys, and then NEVER let them play with them.

Instead, he would hog them all for himself.

A car-and-racing-track set went straight into the garage for Monty to amuse himself with alone. Moe and Curly were not even allowed to look at it **"in case they broke it with their eyes"**.

A train set suffered a similar fate. It was kept under lock and key in the attic. And Father had hidden the key!

A remote-controlled fighter plane would be taken to the park, and only flown by Monty. Although when he crashed into the park keeper he handed the remote control to his sons so they had to take the blame.

However, Monty's favourite toy in the world was **BRICKO.** **BRICKO** is a line of building sets, with bricks made of different-coloured plastic. Monty bought his two sons boxes and boxes of the stuff.

"Merry Christmas, chaps!" Monty would announce.

"Thank you, Father!" they would reply, their little eyes lighting up with glee. Then, as soon as they had unwrapped it and exclaimed, **"BRICKO!** BRILLIANT!"**,** the man would snatch it back from them.

"Don't you worry, chaps. Father will put this one together for you!"

With that, he would disappear up to his bedroom and start building.

Over the years, Monty had collected every single **BRICKO** set.

A **BRICKO** Queen Victoria

A **BRICKO** clog

A **BRICKO** jelly

A **BRICKO** beard

A **BRICKO** gerbil

A **BRICKO** mobility scooter

A **BRICKO** cactus

A **BRICKO** marshmallow

A **BRICKO** microwave oven

A **BRICKO** poop*

Mr Monopolize was bananas about **BRICKO**. He would snap the bricks to one another all day.

CLICK! CLICK! CLICK!

And all night.

CLICK! CLICK! CLICK!

If Moe and Curly tried to help snap the bricks together, he would shoo them out of his bedroom.

"BEGONE! **BRICKO** IS ONLY TO BE PLAYED WITH BY GROWN-UPS! NOT CHILDREN!"

Kids love to use **BRICKO** to build their own weird and wonderful creations. Not Monty. No, he followed the impossibly long instruction booklets to the absolute letter. **BRICKO** sets had to be built perfectly to plan.

* **WALLYFACT: BRICKO** poop comes in three different sizes: small, medium and elephant.

One afternoon, Monty Monopolize was on his way home from work at the frozen-pea factory. His job was counting out the peas for each bag: 327. Not one more. Not one less. The man always walked home the long way round so that he could go past the **BRICKO** superstore. That afternoon Monty spotted a gigantic new building-set box that took up the whole of the shop window. It was the largest set **BRICKO** had **ever** produced.

One million pieces!

The Earth.

Yes! A gigantic model of

the Earth!

Monty's eyes widened with delight. This was the most detailed model **BRICKO** had ever produced. Every continent, every ocean, every mountain range was represented. There were people, animals, fish swimming in the seas. Even Monty and the family home were there. And the model wasn't that much smaller than the real Earth. This could be Monty Monopolize's **million-piece masterpiece!** He had to have it!

So he waited until Christmas and announced to his sons, "This year I have bought you two boys a joint present."

"Is it **BRICKO?**" asked Moe, already knowing the answer.

"Just you wait and see."

"It is **BRICKO,** though, isn't it?" added Curly, rolling his eyes.

"Well, don't spoil it for yourselves! But, yes, it is. DARLING!" he called out. **"BRING IN THE PRESENT!"**

Moira Monopolize, the boys' mother, was so fed up with her husband's **BRICKO** obsession that she rarely uttered a word. So, without saying a thing, Mother pushed the biggest gift you've ever seen into the living room. The box was the size of a double-decker bus. Using all her might, she slid it through the door.

The family cat, Bricko, leaped out of the way...

"MIAOW!"

...as the box hit the **BRICKO** Christmas tree.

DOINK!

The plastic tree came crashing down on her husband's head.

WHOOSH!

BOINK!

Breaking into pieces.

"ARGH! CAREFUL!" he shouted as his sons chuckled to themselves.

"Ha! Ha! Ha!"

For a brief moment, a flicker of a smile crossed Moira's mouth. She must have knocked over the Christmas tree on purpose!

Naughty Mummy! thought the boys.

"MERRY CHRISTMAS!" announced Father. "ON THE COUNT OF THREE YOU MAY UNWRAP! THREE, TWO..."

"Father, why don't you just open it?" asked Moe.

"Cut out the middleman," added Curly.

"Moe, Curly, I have absolutely no idea what you mean! This is YOUR Christmas present. And I want you two boys to enjoy it! ONE! UNWRAP!"

The boys shook their heads, and reluctantly went to work ripping the wrapping paper off.

RIP! RAP! RUP!

Finally, the box was revealed in all its glory.

"**BRICKO** Earth?" uttered Moe, not quite believing what he was reading.

"One million pieces!" added Curly. "That is NUTS!"

"Well, I think you have both enjoyed your Christmas present long enough. Darling, please take the box upstairs to our bedroom!"

Mother shook her head in disbelief, and pushed the box back out of the living room, running over her husband's foot in the process.

"OUCH!" he cried.

Once again, she smirked to herself.

Just then Moe whispered something in Curly's ear.

"What's that?" demanded Father.

"Nothing!" chirped the boys together.

"You two are up to something!"

"Never!" replied Moe.

"Enjoy playing with our latest present, Father!" added Curly.

"Mmm. Yes. I will! Merry Christmas, one and all!"

That Christmas morning, Monty set to work. He banned anyone from entering the bedroom, putting up a sign on the door made with **BRICKO** bricks that read:

Monty laid out all the hundreds of instruction booklets and thousands of individual bags of plastic bricks meticulously on the floor. This operation needed military precision. Even if it was with only an army of one. But, as soon as they heard their father take his first pee break, the two boys crawled over to his bedroom door. The brothers had timed their father's pees, and knew he took exactly twenty-seven seconds to pass water. So, with Father in the bathroom, Moe slid into the man's bedroom on his tummy, while Curly studied a stopwatch. Curly counted down from twenty-seven so his brother would be out of the bedroom in the nick of time.

"Twenty-seven, twenty-six, twenty-five, twenty-four..." he whispered.

The boys' plan was simple. Moe needed to find the smallest piece of the **BRICKO** Earth set.

"Twenty-three, twenty-two, twenty-one, twenty, nineteen…"

One that would take time for his father to realise that it was missing.

"Eighteen, seventeen, sixteen, fifteen…"

One that came right at the end of the building process.

"Fourteen, thirteen, twelve, eleven…"

So they could teach their father a lesson.

"Ten, nine, eight, seven…"

BINGO! Moe found it! A tiny plastic brick of Monty himself!

"Six, five, four…"

Moe slid out of their father's bedroom, just catching his foot on one of the **BRICKO** models.

"Three, two, **one!**" hissed Curly.

Just then their father returned from his pee. The man noticed that the life-sized **BRICKO** model of Queen Victoria was wobbling. He looked around the room with suspicion. Seeing nobody there but him, he shrugged and returned to building the Earth.

CLICK! CLICK! CLICK!

Night and day, brick after brick after brick was snapped together.

CLICK! CLICK! CLICK!

As the model grew and grew, Monty had to knock down walls in the house to accommodate the huge model.

BOOSH!

All this time, his wife looked on, shaking her head at the MADNESS. Meanwhile, the boys kept their secret from their father.

"Psst! Moe, have you still got it?" asked Curly as he lay on the bottom bunk.

"Shush! Yes, I have!" replied Moe as he lay on the top

bunk. "I have it right here!" He opened his hand and showed his brother the treasure. The one tiny brick of Father that he'd taken.

Now all they had to do was play a waiting game.

Days, weeks and months went by until the entire house had been taken over by this **gigantic model** of the Earth. Monty had not just demolished the walls, but all the floors of the house to accommodate his masterpiece. The South Pole was at the very bottom of the house in the cellar, with the North Pole at the very top, poking out of the roof. Now Monty was standing on a very tall ladder, on the home straight.

CLICK! CLICK! CLICK!

Just a few more bricks to snap together until **BRICKO** Earth was complete.

CLICK! CLICK! CLICK!

It had taken from Christmas Day to Christmas Day.

An entire year!

The two boys could hardly contain their glee at what was about to come.

CLICK! CLICK...

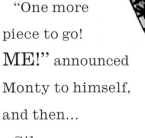

"One more piece to go! ME!" announced Monty to himself, and then...

Silence.

"Where is it? NO! This can't be! There's a piece missing!"

He called down to his sons,

"HAVE YOU SEEN A **BRICKO** PIECE ANYWHERE?"

"NO!" they chirped together. Moe still had the tiny piece hidden in his sweaty little hand.

So, under Monty's orders, the rest of the family began the hunt for the "missing" **BRICKO** piece.

"UNDER THE RUG!" Father called out from up his ladder.

They checked under the rug.

"ON TOP OF THE BOOKSHELF!"

They checked on top of the bookshelf.

"INSIDE THE CAT!"

They picked up Bricko the cat and shook her a little.

"MIAOW!"

But, of course, there was no sign of it in her either.

Soon poor Mother looked exhausted, and Moe and Curly began to feel guilty that she'd been sent on this wild-goose chase.

"PSST! MOTHER!" whispered Moe. "Shush! Don't tell Father, but look…"

The boy opened his hand to reveal the tiny **BRICKO** Monty.

Moira beamed from ear to ear, clearly delighted her sons were playing a trick on their annoying father.

"What are you all conspiring about down there?" demanded Monty.

"NOTHING!" lied the boys.

Father didn't believe them. He slid down his ladder.

W H I Z Z !

"You know where the final piece is, boys!" he said

accusingly when he reached the bottom.

"No, we don't!" they replied.

"HOLD OUT YOUR HANDS!"

he barked.

Curly opened his hands. Nothing.

"NOW YOU!"

Moe was sweating. He opened his left hand, keeping the other behind his back. Nothing.

Then he swapped the piece into the other hand behind his back and opened his right hand. Nothing.

"Both at the same time!" ordered Father.

The boy sighed. He looked to his mother, who nodded. Reluctantly Moe opened his hand.

There was the missing piece.

"I knew it!" exclaimed Monty. "We will have words, you and I! Wicked, wicked child! Now I will finish my masterpiece!"

Father went to snatch the last piece of plastic, but, just before he could, his wife picked it up, popped it in her mouth and swallowed.

GULP!

The boys burst out laughing.

"HA! HA! HA!"

"REGURGITATE THAT **BRICKO** PIECE AT ONCE!" Monty boomed.

Mother shook her head as her sons took her by the hands.

"COME ON, MUM! LET'S NOT LET HIM HAVE IT!"

Together the three raced up the ladder.

CLUNK! CLUNK! CLUNK!

Monty charged up after them.

CLUNK! CLUNK! CLUNK!

"COME BACK THIS INSTANT!" he shouted.

They were now at the very top of the wobbling ladder. The only way to get away from Monty was to run right across the **BRICKO** Earth.

"DON'T YOU DARE!" bawled Monty. "STEP AWAY FROM MY CREATION!"

"It was actually meant to be our present!" shouted Curly.

"Well, er, um, technically it is!" blustered Father.

"Then we can do what we like with it!" replied Moe.

Still holding their mother's hands, the three ran across the North Pole, doing their best to avoid the **BRICKO** polar bears.

Monty jumped on to the Earth in pursuit. The weight of all four of them on the model made it rock out of its base.

TRUNDLE!

Suddenly the Monopolize family were running along the Earth as it rolled across the floor.

It smashed through the back wall of the house...

CRASH!

...spun through the garden and rolled over the garden shed, crushing it instantly.

CRUNCH!

It was like being part of some kind of circus act, trying to stay upright on this giant globe. But, as fast as Monty went, he couldn't catch up with his family. They ran down through Greenland, Scandinavia, Russia, China, India, Australia, New Zealand, until they hit the South Pole. Then they ran up through South America, America, Canada and back up to the North Pole again.

The Earth was rolling through garden fences...

SMASH!

...demolishing walls...

BOOSH!

...even flattening houses.

CRUNDLE!

Soon the Monopolize family found themselves speeding down a steep hill. The **BRICKO** Earth rolled faster and faster, and as it did so it began to rattle.

RITTLE! RATTLE! RUTTLE!

Soon, like all **BRICKO** models, it began to come apart. Plastic bricks every colour of the rainbow showered all over the road.

CLUNK! CLUNK! CLUNK!

"NOOOOO!" screamed Monty.

"JUMP!" shouted Moe. Still clasping his mother's hand, he and Curly took their chances, and leaped off into a hedge.

RUSTLE!

RUSTLE!

RUSTLE!

Still Monty sped on down the hill, the bricks coming loose here, there and everywhere.

CLUNK! CLUNK! CLUNK!

A giant hole appeared on the surface of the **BRICKO** Earth, through which Monty tumbled.

WHOOSH!

"ARGH!"

Father was now inside the model of the Earth, being tossed around like a ball in a Bingo spinner.

DOOMPH!

DOOMPH!

DOOMPH!

Then the **BRICKO** Earth smashed into a little car that was chugging up the road.

BANG!

"WATCH WHERE YOU ARE GOING WITH THAT PLANET!" cried the man inside, a newsagent named Raj.

The model shot up over the car, high into the air...

WHOOSH!

...and began separating into hundreds of thousands of pieces.

CRACK! CRUCK! CRICK!

"ARGH!" cried Monty as he tumbled towards the ground.

W H O O S H !

BOOF!

Father hit the ground hard...

SPLAT!

...as an avalanche of plastic bricks landed on top of him...

CLICK!

CLACK!

CLUCK!

...burying him alive.

His family ran over to him.

"FATHER!" shouted the boys.

There was no answer.

Then Mother put her finger in her ear and began making bizarre honking noises. Her sons looked on in amazement as she began summoning something from the depths of her tummy.

"HONK! HOO! HUH!"

Eventually the **BRICKO** piece she had swallowed shot out of her mouth...

W H I Z Z !

...and landed in the palm of her hand.

TING!

She then picked up the tiny plastic model of her husband and dropped it on top of the mountain of **BRICKO** pieces under which he was buried.

"One more won't hurt!" she remarked.

Moe and Curly laughed.

"HA! HA!"

"Father will be fine! He can dig his way out. So, shall we head home?" she asked, taking her boys by their hands.

"Mum?" said Moe.

"Yes?"

"I don't think we have a home any more."

"It's been smashed to pieces!" added Curly.

"You are right – it has."

The three thought for a moment.

"I know!" exclaimed Moe. "We can build a new one!"

"OUT OF **BRICKO!**" added Curly.

"PERFECT!" agreed Mother.

Behind them, they failed to see Monty Monopolize's hand emerge from the mountain of plastic bricks. Father was alive!

Immediately Moe and Curly set to work. They used all the **BRICKO** bricks they had in order to build a whole new house. The boys had oodles of fun, not following any boring booklets, but instead making it up as they went along.

So, if you ever pass by a crazy multicoloured castle made entirely of little plastic bricks, chances are it belongs to the Monopolize family. Mother, Moe, Curly and Bricko the cat couldn't be happier in their BONKERS new home.

You may even spot a tiny shed also made out of plastic bricks in the garden. In case you were wondering, that is where Monty Monopolize now lives. And the annoying father is only allowed two **BRICKO** bricks to play with.

CLICK!

CLICK!

HARRIET HURRY

The mother with a need for speed

WHIZZ

ZOOM

WHOOSH

HARRIET
HURRY

YOU HAD TO WATCH OUT when Harriet was about. The
long-limbed lady always rode her bike far too fast. The
mother of six children, all girls, she dressed in cream
silk blouses and long, flowing, flowery skirts, topped off
with a feathered felt hat. Each morning, Harriet piled

all six of them on to her old-fashioned lady's bicycle
to race them to school. Despite her proper appearance,
Harriet was a **SPEED DEMON.** And the route from the
country house where the Hurry family lived to school
was downhill. So, with all the weight of her six children
on the bicycle, Harriet could reach eye-watering speeds.

She would overtake sports cars...

WHIZZ!

...speed through red lights...

WHOOSH!

...soar over speed bumps...

ZOOM!

...take short cuts through
hedges...

RUSTLE!

...and perform a triumphant wheelie
when they finally reached the school.

WHIRR!

To understand this obsession with speed, we need to
go back to when Harriet was a baby herself. At her
birth, she shot out of her mother's tummy super-fast. So
super-fast that the midwife couldn't catch her. The poor

lady was like a goalkeeper trying to catch a speeding football booted by a star striker.

SPOT THE DIFFERENCE

Baby Harriet soared over the head of the midwife...

WHOOSH!

...sailed out of a window...

ZOOM!

...luckily landing in an empty pram idling outside the hospital.

DOOMPH!

The force of Baby Harriet's landing made the pram shoot off.

WHIRR!

The seconds-old infant was immediately speeding away from the hospital. As the child's mother screamed from the window of the maternity ward...

"STOP THAT BABY!"

...the newborn sat up in the pram,

cooing with delight to be going so fast.

"GOO! GOO! GAA! GAA!"

The pram rattled off down the road.

RITTLE! RUTTLE! ROTTLE!

It weaved in and out of the path of oncoming

ambulances.

NEE-NAW! NEE-NAW!

Someone must have alerted the **police**, as

in no time three **police officers** on motorbikes

were chasing after Baby Harriet.

One of them shouted at the baby, "STOP, BABY!

OR I WILL PUT YOU UNDER ARREST!"

Baby Harriet was having none of it. Instead of

stopping, she bounced harder and harder on her bottom.

BOINK! BOINK! BOINK!

But trouble was ahead. They were heading straight for

a river at colossal speed. The baby bounced harder and

harder still. **BOINK! BOINK! BOINK!**

The pram hit the riverbank so fast that it soared over the water and landed on the other side.

DOOF!

The **police officers** were not so lucky. Despite revving their engines...

ROARR!

...they weren't going fast enough and plunged into the river.

SPLOSH!

Now there was no stopping Baby Harriet. Up ahead, more **police** had set up a roadblock of **police** cars to stop the runaway baby. There was no way through. Or was there?

A huge smile spread across Baby Harriet's face when she saw the **police** cars lined up ahead of her. She bounced and bounced up and down on her bottom...

BOINK! BOINK! BOINK!

...making the wheels of the pram spin until they were nothing but a blur.

WHIRR!

The **police officers'** faces turned to panic as they realised the runaway baby was not going to stop.

They closed their eyes as she leaned back and the front wheels of the pram lifted. It was a pram wheelie! Or "preelie"!*

Then DISASTER STRUCK. The back wheels of the pram hit the bonnet of a **police** car.

SLAM!

The pram somersaulted through the air, performing a loop-the-loop.

Baby Harriet wasn't the least bit frightened. In fact, she was having a whale of a time! The five-minute-old tot cooed with delight as she sailed upside down over the heads of the **police officers.**

"WOOOH!"

WHOOSH!

"BABY OVERHEAD!"

POLICE

* See your **Walliamsictionary** for the full definition. It has one billion made-up words for you to enjoy.

By some miracle, the pram hit the road on all four wheels at the other side of the **police** roadblock.

DONK!

It was now going faster than ever.

ZOOM!

Just up ahead was a **Formula One** racing track. The pram managed to speed through the entrance...

WHIZZ!

...swerve round the barriers...

SCREECH!

...before racing along the track.

Baby Harriet weaved through the pack of racing cars, taking the corners on the inside and speeding like never before.

ZOOM!

The finish line was in sight.

The baby bounced up and down as hard as she could on her bottom...

BOINK! BOINK! BOINK!

...and when the chequered flag was waved...

WHOOSH!

...Baby Harriet in her pram took first place!
The crowd cheered.

"HURRAH!"

The furious **Formula One** drivers had to
stand by and watch a newborn baby
lift the trophy, before spraying
champagne all over them.

FIZZ!

That glorious moment
made headlines all over
the world:

BABY IS NUMBER ONE!

FORMULA ONE'S YOUNGEST-EVER WINNER!
ONLY TEN MINUTES OLD!

BABY BANNED FOR LIFE FROM DRIVING

Forty years later, that baby had grown up and become a mother to six children. She named them after famous male **Formula One** racing drivers, even though all of them were girls.

Alain   James   Ayrton   Lewis   Niki   Jackie

Formula One racing was all that Harriet watched on the television, much to the displeasure of her ageing cardiganed husband, whom she named **"the Tortoise"**.

Harriet had the racing on long into the night and would shout at the TV if her favourite driver was not going fast enough.

"COME ON, MAN, FOR GOODNESS' SAKE!"

"PUT YOUR GREAT FAT FOOT DOWN!"

"I COULD CYCLE FASTER THAN THAT, YOU BUFFOON!"

She would wake up the whole house with her shouts.

Not that her six daughters had any interest in *SPEED.* They hated the fact that their mother always cycled them to school so fast. The girls had to balance like a **CIRCUS ACT** on her bicycle, which she had named *"LIGHTNING".*

Despite their pleas for her to slow down...

"NOO!"

"HELP!"

"TOO FAST!"

"MAMA!"

"SLOW THE HEAVENS DOWN!"

"ARGH!"

...Mama would pedal harder and harder and harder.

WHIRR! WHIRR! WHIRR!

When she reached *TOP SPEED,* Harriet would holler,

"FASTER! FASTER! RAH! RAH! RAH!"

She treated the school run as if it were a race, a race she had to win at all costs. If Harriet didn't beat every other mother and father, she would be in an almighty **FUNK** all day. It meant that she would pedal harder the next morning, and the ordeal of the school run for the

girls would become worse and worse. The six had to cling
on to **LIGHTNING** for dear life:

   Alain to the front wicker basket...

   James to the front wheel guard...

   Ayrton to the handlebars...

   Lewis to the back wheel guard...

   Niki on the back of the saddle...

   And **Little Jackie** to **Niki's** shoulders.

   The girls thought each day
might be their last.

   So, one morning when they'd

arrived at school after *LIGHTNING* had had a near-
miss with a fire engine, the Hurry children decided that
enough was enough.

They had to do something about Mama.

Each of the girls had a different idea.

Alain was the oldest, and so went first: "We should bury
LIGHTNING in the rose garden!" she exclaimed.

But her younger sisters reckoned their mother would
find it in no time, and that they would end up
having to go to school with soil on their bottoms.

James was the second oldest. She
thought she had a good idea,

suggesting, "Why don't we tie Mama's bootlaces together so she can't cycle so fast?"

The girls soon imagined the bicycle crashing, and all of them landing in a giant heap on the ground. Not fun. Not fun at all.

Ayrton was next. She thought that "puncturing one or both of *LIGHTNING'S* tyres would definitely slow Mama down"!

However, Harriet had trained her daughters to be her back-up team, like **Formula One** drivers have. The girls would be ordered to change *LIGHTNING'S* tyre in less than **three seconds** flat. Mama would check the stopwatch as her six helpers went to work.

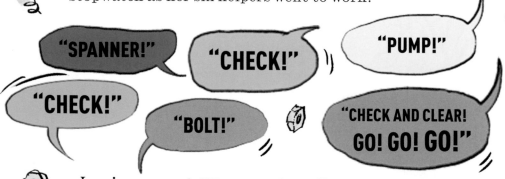

"SPANNER!"
"CHECK!"
"PUMP!"
"CHECK!"
"BOLT!"
"CHECK AND CLEAR! GO! GO! GO!"

Lewis proposed, "If we saved up all our pocket money to buy Mama a horse, then she could ride us all to school on that instead?"

This was judged to be the worst idea so far. Mama would be sure to ride the horse as if she were a jockey at the **GRAND NATIONAL.** A racehorse would be infinitely more dangerous than a bicycle. And, of course, bicycles don't **BITE** bottoms, like some horses have been known to do.*

Niki's suggestion that they "sneak out of bed in the middle of the night, armed with glue pens to coat the whole road with glue to slow down *LIGHTNING*" didn't even warrant a response.

All eyes turned to **Little Jackie.** "I know!" began the youngest of the sisters. "I will join the **police** and then I can arrest Mama for speeding!"

This was greeted with howls of laughter!

"HA! HA! HA!"

"HO! HO! HO!"

"HEE! HEE! HEE!"

The Hurry sisters had never heard anything so ABSURD.

"LISTEN!" shouted **Little Jackie** over the guffaws.

---

* **WALLYFACT:** The worst offender in terms of a horse biting bottoms is world-record holder **Nibble,** a Shetland pony who once bit the bottoms of 347 people at a summer fair in 1981. And I still have the bite marks to prove it.

"I can go to the **police** station straight after school and ask to become a **police officer**."

"YOU CAN'T JOIN THE **POLICE**, LITTLE JACKIE!" mocked **Alain**. "You're far too young! You have to be a grown-up to join the **police!**"

Being the oldest, **Alain** liked to think of herself as the boss. The other four chimed in, following suit.

"WHAT A SILLY IDEA!" "AS IF!" "JACKIE'S JUST A BABY!"

"SHE BARELY COMES UP TO MY KNEES!"

"BE QUIET, THE LOT OF YOU, AND LISTEN!" shouted **Little Jackie,** who was by far the feistiest of the six. Her sisters fell silent. "If we all sit on each other's shoulders, with me at the top, I can pass myself off as a grown-up!"

This stumped the others for a moment.

"But the **police officer** will know it's just six kids on each other's shoulders," reasoned **James**.

The others all murmured in agreement.

"MURMUR!"

"MURMUR!"

"MURMUR!"

"I'VE ALREADY THOUGHT OF THAT!" announced **Little Jackie.** "We borrow Mama's super-long dressing gown! And, look, I've got **this!**"

The girl produced a joke-shop moustache that she'd received in her stocking at Christmas. She smoothed down her hair and stuck on the moustache.

Suddenly, **Little Jackie's** plan didn't seem so stupid after all.

So it was set in motion.

There was much arguing about who should go at the bottom. No one wanted to go at the bottom. **Little Jackie** took charge and managed to convince **Alain** that "being on the bottom is the most important job of all as you are the **legs of the operation**".

That swung it!

The sisters arranged themselves vertically in order of age. It was like a family of **CIRCUS** acrobats as, one by one, they climbed on to each other's shoulders.

At the bottom, **Alain** loved the fact that she, and she alone, chose where the legs would take them.

They were her legs, after all.

Then it was **James** on **Alain's** shoulders.

Next, **Ayrton** was on **James's**.

Then **Lewis** on **Ayrton's.**

Further up, **Niki** was on **Lewis's** shoulders.

Finally, **Little Jackie** was perched at the very top.

Mum's fuchsia-pink dressing gown turned out to be the perfect length for this ruse. It ended just above **Alain's** knees. So, one windy morning before Mama and Papa woke up, the six sisters wobbled their way out of their country house, and down to the local **police** station.

Walking down the street, **Little Jackie** got some strange looks, what with being impossibly tall, and having the face of a girl with a joke-shop moustache stuck on, not to mention the long, pink, *frilly* dressing gown. But she styled it out by peering down her nose at passers-by.

Finally, the tower of girls made it all the way to the local **police** station. Standing on duty behind the counter that morning was an especially stern-looking **police officer,** PC Staid.

On seeing this vision in front of her, her **beady** eyes nearly burst out of her head.

"YES?" barked Staid.

The girls were so taken aback by the bark that they very nearly lost their balance.

WIBBLE! WOBBLE! WABBLE!

"Erm, um, hello..." began **Little Jackie,** her joke-shop moustache coming loose as her face beaded with sweat.

"ARE YOU DRUNK?" demanded Staid.

"No!" replied the girl, putting on a deep **manly** voice. "I just had a pineapple juice."

"That's what they all say! Are you here to report a crime?"

"No! There is a big problem with speeding in this town and I want to sign up to be a **police officer!**"

Staid shook her head. "You look a little young to be a **police officer!**"

"Told you so!" hissed **Alain** from the bottom.

Little Jackie silenced her sister with a sharp shhh under her breath.

"OUCH!"

"What was that?" demanded Staid.

"Just a *bottom burp!*" replied the girl, trying to make her voice sound even **deeper** than before.

"It didn't sound like a *bottom burp*. It sounded like a cry of pain!"

"It was a big one! So it was a little bit painful!" she lied. "My bottom does that sometimes. **Yelps!**"

The PC rolled her eyes. "Well, if you want to be a **police officer,** you have to fill out this form here."

She passed a piece of paper across the desk. The hands that were poking out of the sleeves of the dressing gown were actually **Ayrton's.** As **Ayrton's** face was hidden behind the dressing gown, she couldn't see where the form was. So, when she reached out her hand to grab it, she missed.

Not once.

Not twice.

But three times.

After accidentally grabbing PC Staid's hand, when **Ayrton** finally got hold of the piece of paper, she managed to scrunch it into a ball.

~SCRUNCH! ~

"You **are** drunk!" accused Staid again.

"No! No! Just a tiny bit clumsy," lied **Little Jackie.**

"Clumsy isn't good for a **police officer.** You might drop your truncheon! And then where would we be? **ANARCHY!"**

"Please can I have another form?" asked **Little Jackie.** "And this time I would really appreciate it if you could put it straight into my hand!"

Staid sighed theatrically as grown-ups often do, and did what the girl asked. **"HUMPH!"**

"Thank you so much!" replied **Little Jackie,** turning to go.

"Not so fast!" barked Staid.

Oh no! thought the girl. *What now?* "Yes?"

"Why do you want to be a **police officer** so much?"

"It's my mama."

"What about your mama?" asked Staid.

"She *SPEEDS!"*

"Does she now? How fast are we talking?"

"Well, once she went so fast that she broke the sound barrier. **BOOM!"**

"That is fast."

"I told you it was fast."

"I know, but I didn't know it was that fast."

"Should have been paying close attention. I did say fast!"

Staid sighed again. "HUMPH! Well, good luck with your application, Mr...?"

"Little Jackie!" replied the girl, her joke-shop

moustache now flapping off. "I mean..."

"Good luck, Mr Jackie Little!"

"Goodbye!" mumbled Little Jackie. On the way out, the tower of girls knocked over a stand, scattering leaflets everywhere...

FLUTTER!

...tripped over a **police** dog...

"WOOF!"

...and knocked over a **policeman** and the robber he had handcuffed.

"OOF!"

Staid shook her head in disbelief.

The plan hadn't quite gone to... er... plan. Even so, **Little Jackie** filled out the **police** application form and sent it off. To her and her five sisters' great surprise, the very next day **Little Jackie** received an official letter from PC Staid.

DEAR MR JACKIE LITTLE,

THANK YOU FOR COMING INTO THE POLICE STATION. I HAVE GOOD NEWS. YOU HAVE BEEN ACCEPTED INTO THE POLICE. CONGRATULATIONS. YOU WILL BEGIN FIRST THING TOMORROW WITH TRAFFIC REGULATIONS. PLEASE REPORT TO ME AT THE POLICE STATION AT DAWN.
  YOURS POLICELY,
  PC STAID (THE ONE WITH THE BEADY EYES)

The next morning, the tower of girls wobbled excitedly all the way down to the **police** station. As the sun rose over the town, they were met by PC Staid, who immediately began to explain how a **SPEED GUN** worked. It was a device that **police officers** use to point at vehicles they think are going over the speed limit.

"So, you just point that at the bicycle?" asked the girl.

Staid spat out her tea.

SPLURT!

"BICYCLE?" she exclaimed.

"Yes, my mama **SPEEDS** on her bicycle!"

"We normally use this on cars and motorbikes and the like. We have never, ever, ever stopped someone on a bicycle for speeding!"

"Trust me. I did say fast."

"That you did," admitted the PC.

"And Mama can pedal a great deal faster than any car or motorbike!"

"Well then, we must set a **SPEED TRAP** for later."

That is exactly what they did. It was decided that the best time would be when Mama would be returning to school that afternoon to pick the girls up.

So the sisters sneaked out of school early, and arranged themselves on top of each other, before putting on their **police** outfit. This was a cap, which was far too big for **Little Jackie's** little head, and a very, very, very long police jacket that PC Staid had kindly provided. The **police officer** met the new recruit, PC **Jackie Little,** just outside the school gates. As the bell rang for the end of school...

DRING!

...they hid in a bush, and Staid handed **Little Jackie** – well, of course, really **Ayrton** – the speed gun, which she immediately dropped.

CLUNK!

When the tower of girls and Staid both tried to pick it up at the same time, their heads banged together.

CLONK!

Eventually, they got into their hiding place, and not a moment too soon, because in the distance they could see Mama racing down the road on **LIGHTNING.**

At first, she and her bicycle were little more than a tiny blur on the horizon. Then the blur became bigger and bigger as she sped nearer and nearer.

Mrs Harriet Hurry did not disappoint.

Pedalling harder than ever, the mummy in a hurry cycled straight over the roof of a sports car...

ZOOM!

...jumped over a motorbike as if she were part of a display team...

WHOOSH!

...and smashed through a fruit-and-vegetable stall, hurling food everywhere.

SPLAT! SPLUT! SPLOT!

"OI!"

Then, with a big grin on her face, Mama took to the final straight. She pedalled **LIGHTNING** as if she were competing for a gold medal at the Olympics.

"FASTER! FASTER! RAH! RAH! RAH!" she cried.

Still hiding in the bush, Staid shouted, "NOW!"
Ayrton pressed the button on the *SPEED GUN*.

CLICK!

Mama was going at such an impossible speed that the *SPEED GUN* actually exploded.

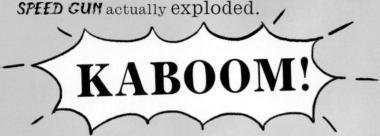

KABOOM!

The sound of the explosion was so loud that it shocked everyone, not least Mama. *LIGHTNING'S* front wheel hit the back of an old lady's mobility scooter.

KABOSH!

Harriet Hurry somersaulted through the air with a look of horror on her face. Oh, how she wished she could somehow slow herself down to a stop.

"HELP!" she shouted as *LIGHTNING* crash-landed on to the road and smashed into hundreds of pieces.

CRASH! BANG! WALLOP!

Meanwhile Mama landed on the top of a very tall tree.

TWANG!

The tree swayed with her weight, and as it swung back it propelled her through the air at speed.

WHOOSH!

All of a sudden, Harriet Hurry was flying into the school, and she didn't know how to stop.

"SLOWER! SLOWER! RAH! RAH! RAH!"

It was as if Mama were a pinball, and the school a giant pinball machine.

Her daughters all peeped out from the line of buttons on the long **police officer's** jacket. They watched helplessly as their mother bounced headfirst into the climbing frame…

CLONNNK!

…rebounded on to the clock tower…

KERLANG!

…hit the goal post…

TERFUNK!

…and smacked straight into the swing.

SWINKDONK!

The swing swung her straight through the window of the science block…

SMASH!

…and out through the other side.

SMASH!

The lady then spun round on the roundabout…

WHIRR!

…before flying off to the slide…

PLONKAFONK!

…speeding down it…

RRRUMMMPH!

…and landing upside down in the sandpit.

BOOMPH!

Harriet was half buried, her legs waggling up in the air.

"HELP!" she cried.

"MAMA!" shouted the girls in shock.

"There's something I need to tell you," began **Little Jackie,** turning to PC Staid. "I am not really this tall."

"I had absolutely no idea!" lied the **police officer** with a knowing wink. **Little Jackie** smiled back as one by one the six girls jumped down from each other's shoulders and ran into the school playground to help their mother.

"I AM STUCK!" shouted Mama.

The sisters formed a human chain to yank her out of the sandpit. **Alain** held on to her mother's feet as **James, Ayrton, Lewis, Niki** and finally **Little Jackie** held on to each other.

"HEAVE!" called **Alain,** and they all heaved. But Mama wouldn't budge. Staid dashed over and joined the chain.

"HEAVE!" commanded the **police officer**.

Like a cork coming out of a bottle, Mama popped out of the sand.

POP!

Soon everyone was lying exhausted in a big heap on the ground.

DOOF!

The school doors banged open and the girls poured out.

On seeing the huddle of people lying on the ground, the biggest girl in the school, Tulisa Thunder, shouted...

"BUNDLE!"

Tulisa ran and leaped on top.

"OOF!"

As the kids streamed out of their classrooms, they all joined in too.

"OOMPH!"

"OOOOOF!"

"OOMMFF!"

"HELP!" shouted Mama, trapped at the bottom of the pile.

"EVERYONE OFF THIS INSTANT!" bellowed a squashed Staid. "I WILL GET THE HEADMASTER TO GIVE YOU ALL EXTRA MATHS HOMEWORK!"

That did the trick. The children all piled off as quickly as they'd piled on.

"REVERSE BUNDLE!" shouted Tulisa Thunder from near the bottom of the pile.

A few moments later, the family were all standing in the playground, clearing sand out of every conceivable place: ears, nose, hair, socks, shoes.

"Do you promise never, ever to *SPEED* again, Mama?" asked **Little Jackie.**

Harriet Hurry looked most unhappy, but reluctantly agreed. "YES!" she sighed.

"Say 'I promise'," prompted **Alain.**

"I promise!" repeated Mama.

Staid's beady eye noticed something. She exclaimed, "Madam! You have your fingers crossed behind your back!"

"MAMA!" moaned the girls.

"All right! All right!" snapped Mama, shaking the last grains of sand from out of her bloomers. "I PROMISE! *LIGHTNING* exploded into a billion pieces anyway!" she added.

"Then my work here is done," said the PC.

"We can't thank you enough," said **Little Jackie.**

"You would make a darn fine **police officer,** Mr Jackie Little."

"Thank you," replied the littlest of the littlest girls.

"Come back to the **police** station in ten years' time, and let's see what we can do."

Little Jackie looked disappointed. "That's ages! And I loved being a **police officer.** Please can I stay one? Please!"

Staid looked lost for words. All the girls were now pleading with the PC on their little sister's behalf.

"PLEASE!"

"All right! All right!" blustered Staid. "I will make you the very first **POLICE KID!**"

"YAY!" cried the sisters.

"You didn't have your fingers crossed behind your back?" accused Mama.

"I would not dream of it, madam!" snapped Staid.

"Here!" The lady took off her own **police** hat and placed it on **Little Jackie's** head.

"Farewell, ladies!"

"GOODBYE!" called out the girls.

"And thank you," added **Little Jackie.**

"Thank *you*!" replied Staid, and she paced out of the playground, shaking sand from her socks as she did so.

Mama gathered her girls around her and **hugged** them tight.

"A thousand thank-yous, girls. You taught your mama an important lesson today."

"I hope so," said **Little Jackie.**

"No more *SPEEDING!* No more bicycle!"

"Good, good, Mama," cooed the girls.

"Now, where is the nearest **SKATEBOARD** shop?"

"NOOOOOOOOOOOOO!"
they screamed.

LORD GRANDIOSE

LORD GRANVILLE GRANDIOSE was an upper-class twit. His father before him had been an upper-class twit. And his father before him had also been an upper-class twit. And so on and so forth, going back for hundreds and hundreds of years of twits, twits and more twits.

As was common with upper-class twits, Lord Grandiose lived in a humongous country house called GRANDIOSE HALL. It had been in the family for generations. Passed from twit to twit.

So, what makes an upper-class twit?

Well, **first** of all, Granville didn't laugh exactly. If he found something funny, like the misfortune of poor people, he would snort.

"SNORT! SNORT! SNORT! JOKES!"

Second, because he was rich and posh, Granville thought he could do whatever he liked. As a result, he would constantly belch boisterously when out at restaurants.

"BURP!"

If anyone dared to complain, the twit would instantly buy the restaurant and have them thrown out!

Third, the buttons on his waistcoats were often pinging off as he always ate too much and his tummy grew rounder and rounder daily.

T W O N G !

Fourth, if you peered into one of Granville's ears, you might see what you thought was a pea rolling around inside his head. Do NOT be alarmed. This would, in fact, be his brain.

(R A T T L E !)

Fifth, Granville would point champagne bottles at his servants, and then open them.

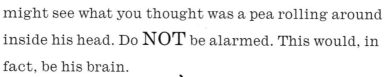

POP! The cork would fly out like a bullet.

WHOOSH! And hit them on the bottom. "OWEE!"

Sixth, if the gates to GRANDIOSE HALL were shut at night, and he couldn't be bothered to get out of the car to open them, he would ram the Rolls-Royce through them at speed.

Z O O M !

KERCHUNG!

Seventh, Granville did absolutely nothing for himself. His butler even had to squirt toothpaste on to his toothbrush, and still he never, ever cleaned his teeth.

SQUIRT?

Eighth, even though he had a remote control for the television set, Granville always rang a bell for the butler to come to change the channel for him.

TINKLE!

"HORSE RACING! NOW!"

Tenth, what happened to **ninth**?

Ninth, oh, there you are.

Counting to ten isn't easy for upper-class twits.

One day, Lord Grandiose met a young lady who was just as **GHASTLY** as he was. Her name was Lady Lavonia Lavish. It was love at first sight. Lavonia was just as

rude, ignorant and bad-tempered as he was, if not more so. She had become famous in upper-class twit circles for firing her maid out of a cannon to the next county when she'd brought her a cold cup of tea.

BANG!

WHOOSH!

"ARGH!"

On hearing this story, Granville knew she was just the gal for him. He spent a fortune throwing a huge party at GRANDIOSE HALL , with mountains of caviar and rivers of

champagne,* and invited only one person: Lavonia.

Instantly, the two twits were smitten, and within a couple of minutes of meeting, had decided to get married. Their wedding, attended by a gaggle of other upper-class twits, made the front cover of society magazine **TWIT!**.

In time, her ladyship gave birth to a baby. His lordship was thrilled. Now he had a son who could one day grow up to be an upper-class twit just like him. The boy would inherit GRANDIOSE HALL and all that came with it.

Humbly, Granville named his son after himself, Granville. In truth, he didn't really know many other names, and the baby boy didn't look much like a Lavonia.

* **WALLYFACT:** Champagne is the most BURPTASTIC drink ever invented. It is always used in burping competitions as it is guaranteed to make the burpers burp dramatically. Burps are judged in three categories. Volume of burp. Length of burp. And, most importantly, stench of burp. The world champion burper is Mr Silus Snurp, an elderly man who can burp for two weeks non-stop.

As soon as he had popped out of his mother's tummy, Baby Granville was handed straight to Nanny.

"Goodbye!" called out his parents, waving, as the baby was wheeled away in a pram.

Just like they hadn't, as babies of upper-class twits themselves, Baby Granville was destined not to see his parents again until he was a grown-up. The tot was kept hidden away in the nursery in a distant wing of GRANDIOSE HALL with Nanny. Fortunately for the child, Nanny was a kindly old dear. She was round and squishy. Perfect for cuddles! Nanny gave the boy all the love in the world, and then some more. There were a few old, battered wooden toys in the nursery, like a rocking horse and a train set, but what the boy loved most was an old leather trunk full of clothes.

This Nanny called

THE DRESSING-UP BOX.

It was a treasure trove of old clothes that had
passed through the Grandiose family for generations.
Old military uniforms, dinner suits, even ballgowns.
As the boy grew up, he and Nanny would while away the
hours with him dressing up to become all sorts of weird
and wonderful characters:

A wizard   A pirate   A knight   A soldier   A cowboy

A doctor   A jockey   A spaceman   A pilot   Even a princess!

The pair never left the nursery, but their adventures took them all over the world.

Meanwhile, for Lord and Lady Grandiose, with their son out of sight he was also out of mind. They barely gave him a thought, and instead got on with the important business of being beastly to the servants. Even though he was living under the same roof, his parents **never** set eyes on Granville Junior in a dozen years.

Instead, Nanny and all the other staff became a family to the boy. The cook would bring him **double helpings** of his favourite puddings, the gardener would show him **worms** and **bugs** from the garden and

the chauffeur would take him for rides around the grounds in the family's vintage Rolls-Royce. As for Nanny, she loved him more and more each day, treating him as if he were her own son.

Over time, Granville Junior began to ask why he'd never met his parents. Nanny would try to bat away these questions with excuses in order not to hurt the boy's feelings. She knew the lord and lady were upper-class twits who had no intention of meeting their son until he was a grown-up. However, on his **twelfth birthday,** the boy decided that enough was enough!

"Nanny," he began, tucking into his boiled egg and soldiers, "please, please, please can you ask my parents if I can finally meet them today?"

"They are very busy with all their upper-class stuff," lied the kindly lady.

"But it's my **birthday!** Don't they even want to wish me a **happy birthday?**"

"Well, I can pass a message on to the maid, and she can tell the housekeeper, and she can tell the footman, and he can tell the butler, and the butler can deliver the message to your parents! It should only take a week or so."

"That is NUTS!" exclaimed the boy.

Nanny sighed and stroked the boy's face tenderly. "Let me see what I can do, young sir."

So a letter from Granville Junior was dispatched, and soon after found its way into the hands of Granville Senior.

"A letter for your lordship," announced the old butler as he entered the impossibly long dining room of GRANDIOSE HALL. A floor-to-ceiling oil painting of *Her Majesty the Queen* dominated the wall.

"Can't you see I'm busy eating my roast beef?" snapped Lord Grandiose. Even though it was still breakfast-time, he liked roast beef so much that he had it three times a day. Lord Grandiose picked up a

Yorkshire pudding and hurled it at the butler. It bonked him bang on the nose.

BOINK!

"Thank you, your lordship!" said the butler.

"SNORT! SNORT! SNORT!"

"What should I do with the letter, sir?"

"Read it for me, you buffoon!"

The butler cleared his throat, and then began. "Dear Papa…"

"I am not your father!" spluttered the lord. "You must be twice, thrice or even frice* my age!"

"The letter is from your son, sir."

"I have a son?"

"Yes, sir!"

"Are you sure?"

"Yes, he was born twelve years ago today!" replied the butler.

* This made-up word is so silly you won't even find it in your Walliamsictionary.

"Oh yes! Rings a bell! Come on! Read on, you silly chump! Don't dilly-dally!"

"Very good, sir."

Dear Papa and Mama, I would very much like to meet you today, please. It is my birthday, after all.
Yours sincerely, your son

finished the butler.

"The impudence!" Lord Grandiose called out to his wife, "Lavonia, darling, I just had a letter from our son. He wants to meet us."

Lady Grandiose was sitting at the opposite end of the impossibly long dining table, about half a mile away from him.

"I CAN'T HEAR YOU! CAN YOU SHOUT?" she called back.

"I SAID, 'OUR SON WANTS TO MEET US!'"

"Oh, what a frightful bore! Do we have to?" sighed Lavonia as she poured some champagne into a saucer for the pair of Siamese cats snaking around her ankles.

"MIAOW!"   "MIAOW!"

The cats lapped up the champagne.

"SLURP!"

"SLURP!"

One toppled over, knocked out cold.

DOOSH!

The other blew off loudly from the bubbles.

PFFT!

"I was really rather hoping we might just bump into him at a cocktail party when he is all grown-up," added Lavonia, completely oblivious to the cat chaos she'd caused.

"I know it's a dreadful drag, darling, but the letter is quite insistent! He wants to meet us today!" he replied.

"Whatever for?" she exclaimed. "I don't think I ever met my parents. No, tell a lie, I bumped into my mother at my father's funeral. Awful woman!"

"I haven't the foggiest."

"Well, it's very selfish of him. I am not sure I ever want to meet anyone so dastardly **selfish!**"

"Beastly of the little brute, I know, but apparently it's his **birthday** today."

"Is it?"

"Yes."

"And what's his name again?"

"Granville!" replied the man.

"I thought that was your name!" she snapped.

"It is!"

"So, you are both called Granville?"

"Yes!"

"Well I never!" she hooted. "You learn something new every day!"

"I will say no to the little twerp!"

"Jolly good show!" agreed the lady.

"Butler!" called out his lordship. "Please tell our son, no. And we would rather he didn't **ever** contact us again."

A look of sorrow crossed the old man's face.

"Are you sure, sir?" he asked.

"THE IMPUDENCE!" yelled his lordship, showering him with a hail of roast potatoes.

DOINK! DOINK! DOINK!

"NOW RUN!" screamed Lord Grandiose, pelting the butler with peas as the poor man darted out of the room.

The butler delivered the sad news to the nursery. The boy's eyes welled with tears. This was the worst **birthday** present ever.

"I am sorry, young sir," whispered Nanny, holding him tight.

Soon the sorrow turned to rage.

"I WILL TEACH THEM A LESSON!" spluttered the boy.

"Don't do anything too hasty!" warned Nanny.

"My stupid parents take afternoon tea in the drawing room every day, right?" demanded the boy.

"Yes, sir," replied the butler.

"Well, then let's make this an afternoon tea those twits will never forget!" he said as a smile spread across his face.

Nanny and the butler shared a worried look, but the boy was adamant. "Nanny! Let's raid

THE DRESSING-UP BOX!"

Granville Junior started putting together a plan. As his parents hadn't seen him since the day he was born, they wouldn't know what he looked like. With the help of the dressing-up box, he could pretend to be any character he wanted.

The question was, who?

"I know who I will be for tea with the lord and lady! *Her Majesty the Queen!*" announced the boy.

Nanny burst out laughing. "HA! HA! HA! Don't be daft!"

"I am not being daft! I bet the *Queen* is the only person they wouldn't say no to!"

The old lady nodded her head. "You're right. Upper-class twits only grovel to royalty!"

"So, if I am dressed as the *Queen*, I can get away with anything! Just you wait and see!"

So, the pair set to work. The boy found a regal gown and some long white gloves in the dressing-up box. Meanwhile, Nanny had a good rummage in the attic and returned with an old wig and a handbag.

Then the pair disguised the two Siamese cats as corgis.

BEFORE

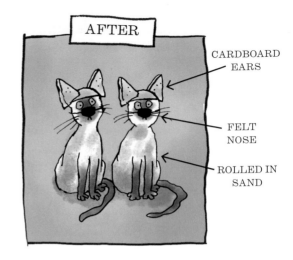

AFTER

CARDBOARD EARS

FELT NOSE

ROLLED IN SAND

Finally, teatime came, and Nanny knocked on the door of the drawing room.

KNOCK! KNOCK! KNOCK!

Lord and Lady Grandiose were sitting in armchairs, scoffing their afternoon tea.

"My lord and lady," began Nanny.

"What do you want, woman?" demanded her ladyship, hurling a cream cake at her.

SPLAT!

It hit her right in the face, though, being a well-trained servant, she continued as if nothing had happened. "A very special guest has arrived unexpectedly at GRANDIOSE HALL . Please be upstanding for *Her Majesty the Queen!*"

The lord and lady looked at each other, aghast. They were not expecting this!

Nanny had got all the servants in on the game. So the chauffeur and the gardener were decked out in gold outfits, pretending to be royal trumpeters heralding the *Queen's* arrival.

BAH-BAH-BAH-BAH- BAH-BAAAH!

In waltzed Granville Junior, looking every inch the *Queen*, dragging the two reluctant "corgis" on leads behind him.

"Good afternoon, peasants!" began *"Her Majesty"* in his poshest voice. The boy had become good at putting on voices in all those years playing dress-up with Nanny. "I hope you don't mind me dropping by for tea and cakes! I was just passing by in my—"

"No! No! Not at all, *Your Majesty*," grovelled Lord Grandiose, kissing the *Queen's* hand.

"What an honour, *Your Royal Highness!*" added Lady Grandiose.

"Yes! It must be for oiks like you!"

Meanwhile, Nanny and all the rest of the staff were huddling in the garden outside the drawing-room window so they could enjoy the show. They stifled their giggles as the boy shuffled over to the tall silver stand of cakes. He took off two huge slices of chocolate cake and placed one on each of his parents' chairs.

The lord and lady looked at each other, with expressions of *What on earth is she doing?*

"You may sit!" commanded the *Queen*. The pair had no choice! This was *Her Majesty the Queen!* They had to obey! So, reluctantly, they sat.

SQUELCH!

SQUELCH!

Now both their bottoms were covered in thick brown goo.

"What an unexpected pleasure this is!" cooed her ladyship.

"I know! Me! *The Queen!* Dropping in on louts like you! Ah, scones! Do you put the jam or the cream on first?" the boy asked, picking up the pots of each.

"As you wish, *Your Majesty!*" replied the lord.

"Very good!" said the *Queen*, spooning up some cream. He pulled back the spoon, and...

SPLAT!

...he hit his mother right in the face with a dollop of cream.

"URGH!"

Then his father.

SPLAT!

"Ladies first! I do hope you
understand!" uttered the Queen.

"Of course, *Your Majesty!*" they replied.

"ON GOES THE JAM!"

SPLAT!
SPLAT!

Both parents now had a faceful of
strawberry jam.

"Thank you, *Your Majesty!*" they cooed.

Nanny and the gang now had their faces pressed up
against the window, looking in.

"HA! HA! HA!"

They couldn't help but laugh. At last, their horrible
bosses were getting their just deserts. Literally!

"Now, any afternoon tea would not be complete
without, of course, the tea," said the Queen

"Of course!" the lord and lady agreed.

"I will pour!"

And pour he did, pouring the milk...

SPLASH!
SPLOSH!

...all over their heads.

"Sugar?"

They both nodded, soaked to the skin and a ghostly shade of white.

Their son smiled his best *queenly* smile, before doing the same with the sugar bowl.

S P R I N K L E !

S P R A N K L E !

"Well, I would love to stay," said the boy as the *Queen* before changing into his real voice, "but I would rather not spend another moment with a pair of STEAMING BOTTOM BOGEYS like you!"

"Thank you so much, *Your Majesty!*" they replied.

Then the boy whipped off his crown and wig, and shouted,

"GOODBYE FOREVER!"

"I never knew the *Queen* wore a wig," remarked Lord Grandiose.

"Me neither," replied Lady Grandiose.

From the outside, Nanny slid open the window, and the boy leaped through it.

The old lady shouted into the room,

"YOU PAIR OF TWITS DON'T DESERVE A LOVELY BOY LIKE HIM!"

before calling out to the chauffeur,

"START THE CAR!"

The chauffeur dashed to the Rolls-Royce and started the engine.

BRUMM!

All the other servants piled in as Nanny and the boy skipped hand in hand to the car, then dived into the back.

The Rolls-Royce raced off.

ZOOM!

They all escaped to a new life, far away from GRANDIOSE HALL on a lovely little farm. Nanny showered the boy with so much love that he never gave a second thought to that ghastly pair again.

What became of the lord and lady? Nothing. The pair of upper-class twits never did a thing for themselves, so they just sat there as the two "corgis" licked the cream and jam off their faces.

"I wonder if *Her Majesty the Queen* will ever come for tea again?" asked Lord Grandiose.

"I do hope so," replied Lady Grandiose. "We should get out of these wet things."

"Yes. We should. Butler! BUTLER!" called out Lord Grandiose. "BUTLER!"

But nobody came.

So the pair waited, and waited, and waited.

Forever.

SUPERMUM!

P AT P ATTERSON NOT ONLY had a **boring** name, she
also had the most **boring** job in the world. She was a
toilet cleaner. Pat lived with her two children on the
top floor of a crumbling tower block. Her youngest
was Spike, a boy of ten, and her oldest, Punk, a girl of

thirteen. Both found their mother **boring**. All she talked about was the toilets she'd cleaned that day.

"With a tough stain like that, there was nothing else for it – I had to get out the scourer!"

So, when she got home from work, Spike would bury his face in a superhero comic as his sister put her headphones over her ears and turned the volume on her music to *BLASTING.*

Being ignored made Mum sad. Looking over her son's shoulder at one of his comic books, she had an idea.

DING!

What if she weren't just **boring** old Mum? What if she were... *SUPERMUM?*

A mum with **superpowers.** Superheroes can be created in all kinds of ways. They might be an **ALIEN** from another planet. They might be a billionaire **inventor.** They might even have been bitten by a **radioactive** insect.

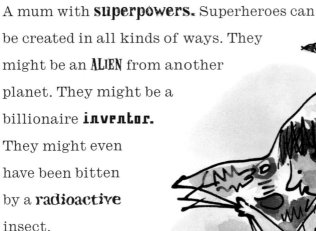

Pat Patterson wasn't blessed with any of these options. Her superhero alter ego would have to be homemade.

As she cleaned bog after bog all day, Pat daydreamed about how she could transform into **SUPERMUM.** Superheroes need weapons. The famous ones have shields, hammers, web shooters, lassos, suits of armour, invisible planes, even shark-repellent spray. Not having any of these, Pat found inspiration in her toilet-cleaning implements.

Pat's **brush, mop** and **bucket** could now be **SUPERMUM'S magic** weapons.

The **bucket** could be

The **mop** would be renamed

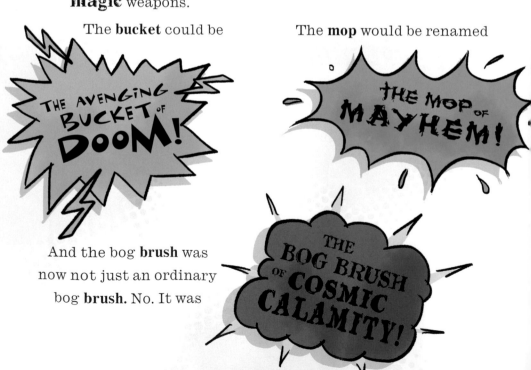

And the bog **brush** was now not just an ordinary bog **brush.** No. It was

Pat didn't know what any of these things really meant, but they sounded **COOL.**

One day at work, when no one was about, Pat practised her quick change. Superheroes had to be good at quick changes. There would be no warning of when a school bus might be dangling over the side of a bridge, or of an aeroplane losing a wing, or a cat getting stuck up a tree. So Pat darted into a bog cubicle, whipped off her cleaning apron and whisked it over her shoulders as a cape. Then she poked two eye holes in her hairband with a pencil, and put it on her face as a mask. She flung open the door fast!

She was **SUPERMUM!** With her three mighty magic weapons, she attacked the hundreds of bogs she had to clean, like never before.

BiSH!

BASH!

BoSH!

As **SUPERMUM,** it was as if Pat really did have special powers. The bogs were cleaned in record time.

"TAKE THAT, TOILET!" she cried as she finished the last one. Little did she know that her dreaded boss, Miss Scowl, was waiting outside the cubicle.

"PAT!" barked Scowl. "WHAT ARE YOU DOING?"

"Sorry, Miss Scowl!" replied Pat meekly.

"PUT THAT APRON BACK ON THE RIGHT WAY ROUND. ANYONE WOULD THINK YOU WERE **CRACKERS!**"

"Sorry."

"YOU LOOK LIKE SOME KIND OF POUND-SHOP SUPERHERO!"

"Well, you see, I was just…"

"PAT, YOU ARE NOT FIGHTING SUPERVILLAINS! YOU ARE CLEANING BOGS!"

"I know…"

"NO MORE OF THIS NONSENSE EVER AGAIN!"

Miss Scowl spun round and marched off.

As the door slammed, Pat bowed her head sorrowfully. When she took the apron from her shoulders, she nearly jumped out of her skin. The bog behind her made a **thunderous** noise.

GURGLE?

Then it began to hum and rattle.

RITTLE! RATTLE! RUTTLE!

Pat rubbed her eyes. This couldn't be true!

But it was.

Then the bog next door began to come alive too.

GURGLE?

RITTLE! RATTLE! RUTTLE!

And the next one along. And the next one. And the next. Something **terrifying** was happening, and Pat was not going to stay to find out what it was. She grabbed her mop, bucket and bog brush, and raced out of the toilets.

That night, Pat came back to the top-floor flat to see her grumpy kids **slumped** on the sofa once again. Spike was colouring in some superheroes in a book, while his sister was listening to music so loudly that it could be heard from the bottom floor of the block.

"Mum's home!" called out Pat when she entered the room, but Punk and Spike just grunted.

"HUH!"

"HUH!"

No change there, but she was sure they wouldn't grunt at *SUPERMUM.* Oh no. Not *SUPERMUM!* So Pat hurried to her bedroom, and began putting together a proper superhero costume.

First, she sewed the body of the outfit together from all her tatty old yellow cleaning cloths. When she tried it on, she looked like a giant banana. Next, she painted a *SUPERMUM* logo on her chest with purple paint. As for footwear, Pat decided upon Wellington boots. She didn't have a matching pair – one was red and one was green.

No matter, she thought. It was all part of the mystery of the character. Then a pink bin liner made an excellent plastic cape, while a colourful stripy sock with two holes made the perfect mask. Finally, a pair of Spike's old underpants worn over the suit completed the look. Especially as they were electric blue.

WOW!

Just as Pat was admiring herself in the mirror, she heard a cry from the next room.

"Mum! I lost one of my colouring pens down the back of the sofa!"

It was Spike. So she raced out of her bedroom, put her hands on her hips and, with her pink plastic cape fluttering behind her, declared:

"This sounds like a job for

SUPERMUM!"

"What are you doing, Mum?" demanded Spike.

"I am not Mum! I am SUPERMUM!
Just like a mum, but even more super-duper-wuper!
Step aside! This calls for my MOP OF MAYHEM!"

"You've got a weapon! Cool!" remarked the boy as his
mother grabbed her trusty mop.

"MOP OF MAYHEM! Find the pen!"

She poked around the back of the sofa with the pole
end as Punk sat there with music blaring out of her
headphones.

After a while of poking and finding nothing, *SUPERMUM*
announced, *"Stand back! I am going in!"*

She paced back to the far corner of the
living room. Then took a running jump…

DOINK!

...and dived into the back of the sofa.

PLUNGE!

Punk, who was still slumped on it, was

bounced up into the air...

BOING!

...landing on the floor on her bottom...

THUMP!

...much to her little brother's delight.

"HA! HA! HA!"

Punk just scowled as Mum reappeared with a brown

felt-tip pen in her mouth.

"I actually lost a red one, Mum!" complained Spike.

"It's not 'Mum' – I know nothing of this 'Mum' of
whom you speak. I am **SUPERMUM!**"

"This is so annoying!" snapped Punk.

"Stand back! **SUPERMUM** will risk her life once more
to reunite you with your red colouring pen!"

Then **SUPERMUM** ran all the way down the corridor to

afford herself a longer run-up.

WHIZZ!

DOINK!

PLUNGE!

Her legs waggled up in the air for a while, before...

"GOTCHA! THE PESKY RED PEN IS FOUND! THE UNIVERSE IS SAFE ONCE MORE!"

"FAB!" replied Spike, clearly loving every second of this.

The lady ruffled the boy's hair, and he beamed.

"It's all in a day's work for the most daring do-gooder of them all, the mum that's super-duper-wuper..." **"SUPERMUM!"** she and Spike said together.

"When is **SUPERMUM** coming back?" demanded Spike, so excited that he was bouncing up and down on the spot.

"Wherever and whenever she is needed. All you have to do is... believe!"

"Believe what?" snorted Punk.

"Believe in SUPERMUM!"

"Oh, give it a rest, Mum!" snapped Punk. "It's already getting sooo boring!"

Mum was hurt, and sloped out of the room.

"Why do you always have to be such a downer?" asked Spike.

"Oh, shut up!" snapped his sister. "Shut up" was her answer to everything.

"**SUPERMUM** is ace!" said Spike. "I love her! And I believe in her! One hundred per cent!"

"Well, you are ten, so you are basically still a baby and would believe in anything!" said the girl before putting her headphones back on.

Pat was down, but not out. She was determined to turn her daughter round. One day, she too would believe in **SUPERMUM.**

*

The very next morning, Mum noticed that Punk had accidentally-on-purpose forgotten her sports kit on cross-country-run day. Could she get the kit to the school before the race began?

This was a job for... **SUPERMUM!**

The superhero burst into Punk's classroom.

WHOOSH!

"NEVER FEAR! THE SUPER-DUPER-WUPER MUM IS HERE! IT'S **SUPERMUM!**"

she announced, wearing her costume, the colour of custard.

"Oh no!" sighed Punk, thumping her head down on her desk.

THUNK!

"Who are you and what are you doing in my classroom?" spluttered the flustered teacher, Miss Frazzle.

"I'M **SUPERMUM**! And the good news is this afternoon's cross-country run will be run, Punk! Here is your sports kit you so conveniently forgot!"

she announced, producing a plastic bag from underneath her pink plastic cape.

"MUM!"

"I found it hidden under your bed. It hasn't been washed so is a bit **stinky!**"

"HA! HA! HA!" laughed Punk's classmates.

"OH, SHUT UP!" snapped the girl.

"Do you believe I have **superpowers** yet?" asked **SUPERMUM** hopefully.

"Of course I don't. I am not NUTS!"

"Then how did I get here in record-breaking time?"

Punk thought for a moment. "I dunno. Maybe you got the bus."

"Superheroes don't get buses!" exclaimed **SUPERMUM.** "Unless they are running very late. Well, I would love to stop and chat, but I have superhero-type stuff to do."

"Do you mind awfully taking to the skies now?" asked Miss Frazzle. "I am trying to teach the children about oxbow lakes, and we'd just got to a tricky bit."

"*Of course!*" replied **SUPERMUM**, before turning to the schoolchildren. "*Enjoy the run, kids! Especially you, Punk! ANOTHER JOB WELL DONE BY THE ONE AND ONLY... SUPERMUM!*"

WHOOSH!

With that, she was gone, and immediately the whole class turned their attention to Punk.

"IS THAT YOUR MUM?"

"SHE'S BANANAS!"

"HA! HA! HA!"

Punk put her fingers in her ears, and let her head sink down on to her desk once more.

THUNK!

Pat was determined to make her daughter love **SUPERMUM** just as much as her son did. So she took every opportunity to transform into her superhero alter ego. There were countless times Pat embarrassed her daughter this way.

When Punk was sitting on a wall with her mates, **SUPERMUM** flew down from a tree to tell her, "*YOUR TEA IS READY!*"

Another time, the girl was idling around the supermarket with some school friends, when **SUPERMUM** burst out from behind a display of baked beans, and reminded her, **"DON'T FORGET TO PICK UP SOME PRUNES! YOU KNOW THEY MAKE YOU GO!"**

Worst of all was the moment when Punk was walking along the estate with a boy she really liked. They had just started holding hands when **SUPERMUM** popped her head out of a manhole cover and announced,

"Your room needs tidying right now, young lady! Your stuff is all over the floor! Filthy socks everywhere!"

For Punk, that was IT!

The girl couldn't take any more embarrassment. There could be no more **SUPERMUM.** EVER!

So she **stomped** all the way home, and up flight after flight of stairs to the top floor of the tower block to confront her mother. However, when Punk opened the door, she was surprised to see her little brother in his OWN superhero outfit. Like his mother's, Spike's outfit was homemade.

The boy had on:

A pair of **underpants** over his face as a mask, his eyes peeping out of the pee-pee hole.

A top made from a **cardboard box,** to give the illusion of body armour ("UB" was painted on the box)

A cape made from a **tea towel**

A **plastic bag** covering his bottom

His mother's purple **tights** for leggings

Wellington boots (both left-foot ones, for some unknown reason)

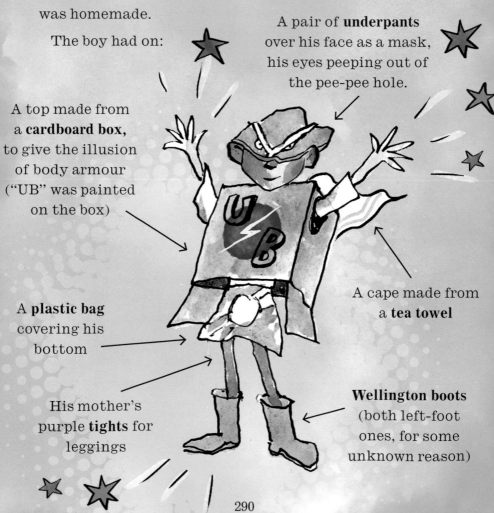

290

"What on earth are you wearing, Spike?" mocked Punk. "You look like a total twit!"

"I am **not** Spike! I am **SUPERMUM'S** superhero buddy –

ULTRABOY!" he announced.

"What does **ULTRABOY** even mean?"

"Dunno. But it sounds cool."

"No, it doesn't! It sounds pants!" she snapped.

"That's what I have wrapped round my head! Look!" The boy proudly displayed his mask of pants, or pants mask.*

"Come on, Punk! You know what Mum says: all you have to do is believe."

"Believe? Not that rubbish again! Why are you even dressed up like that, saddo?"

"Haven't you seen the news?" the boy asked.

"No. What news? Why?"

Just then **SUPERMUM** burst out of her bedroom, her pink plastic cape getting caught in the door. She yanked it out, before putting her hands on her hips and declaring,

"Whatever you do, DON'T put on the TV!"

* **WALLYFACT:** Pants are best worn around the bottom area. But sometimes I wear them on my head, walking down the street, when not enough people recognise me.

Of course, that is exactly what the girl did next,
and Mum knew she would. Punk flicked between the
channels, but every single one of them was showing the
same thing.

"THE WORLD IS UNDER ATTACK," announced a
terrified-looking reporter, **"FROM KILLER TOILETS!**
TOILETS HAVE HAD ENOUGH OF PEOPLE DOING
THEIR BUSINESS IN THEM AND THEY ARE
FIGHTING BACK!"

"WHAT?" exclaimed Punk.
"This is NUTS!"

Could the girl's eyes and ears
be deceiving her? No. She could see, as the whole world
could see: bogs were on the rampage.

Toilets were chasing people down the street in New
York City and gobbling them up.

"ARGH!" screamed another poor victim, his legs
waggling out of the top of one
as he was eaten alive.
went the bogs, their seats

going ᵁᵖ and ᵈₒwₙ as they devoured person after person. Once one had been scoffed, they went straight on to another.

It was the same story everywhere.

In Paris, bogs were going **berserk,** eating up French people as if there were no tomorrow.

"*NON!*"

In Tokyo, those Japanese high-tech bogs were flying through the sky, plucking people off roofs of skyscrapers and chomping on them.

"EEEHHH!"

Then the news turned to London, where none other than Mum's boss, Miss Scowl, was being chased down a street by hundreds of **deadly** bogs. Miss Scowl was screaming for mercy, but the bogs had **no mercy.** They wolfed her down.

"NOOO!" screamed Scowl.

293

burped the bogs.

Punk was unable to stop staring at the TV screen.

"The world is coming to an end!" she cried.

"Unless we stop them! And who better to do that than London's number-one **toilet cleaner** and her two trusty **sidekicks?**"

The TV screen flickered to Trafalgar Square, where the army was advancing to battle the killer bogs.

Guns were being fired.

RAT! TAT! TAT!

Grenades were being thrown.

Missiles were being launched.

WHIZZ!

 But out of the smoke and dust the bogs just kept coming.

SUPERMUM!

Thundering across Tower Bridge.

Bashing into Westminster Abbey.

Smashing down the gates to Buckingham Palace.

SUPERMUM turned to her daughter. "We need you."

"Me?" replied the girl.

"The world needs you."

"You what?"

*"Will you join me – **SUPERMUM** – and **ULTRABOY**, and save the human race from killer bogs?"*

"Well, I... er..." spluttered Punk.

"The fate of all mankind is in our hands!" said **ULTRABOY**.

"Join us, GALACTIC GIRL!"

With that, **SUPERMUM** held up a superhero costume for Punk. It was made up of:

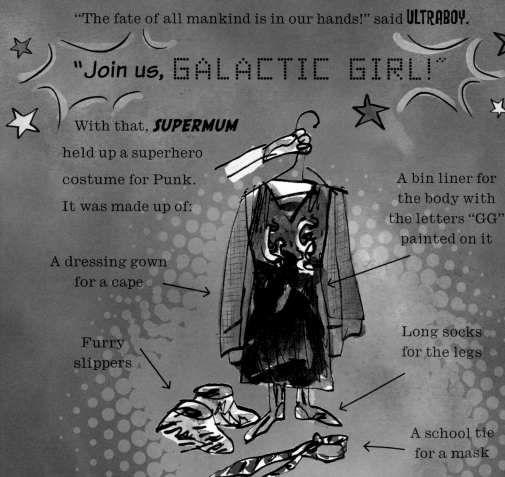

A bin liner for the body with the letters "GG" painted on it

A dressing gown for a cape

Long socks for the legs

Furry slippers

A school tie for a mask

"We are not really superheroes," protested the girl. "We're just an ordinary family who live in a tower block. Don't you have to be an alien or a zillionaire or a mad scientist or something to be a superhero?"

SUPERMUM smiled.

"No. All you need to do is... believe."

"But I can't believe!"

"Of course you can," said Spike. "Close your eyes if that helps."

"It's not going to," replied the girl.

But Punk did as she was told. With her eyes firmly shut, Spike nodded to his mum to put the costume on his sister.

"What are you doing?" she protested, but by the time she opened her eyes it was on.

Punk looked at herself in the mirror. "Actually," she began, "it's not as bad as I thought! I wouldn't go on a date dressed like this, though."

"Well, you aren't going on a date! You're saving the world! So, Galactic Girl, tell me, do you believe? You can only have superpowers if you believe?"

The girl took a breath. "YES! I BELIEVE! SUPERMUM, GALACTIC GIRL IS READY FOR ACTION!"

"YES!" exclaimed ULTRABOY and SUPERMUM.

Then the family of superheroes stood side by side, their capes fluttering heroically.

"So, SUPERMUM?" began Galactic Girl.

"Yes, Galactic Girl?"

"How are we going to defeat these killer bogs?"

It was a reasonable question.

"With my three mighty weapons!" replied SUPERMUM.

"What are they again?" asked Galactic Girl.

"I know the mop one!"

"THE MOP OF MAYHEM!" exclaimed Spike.

"Yes!" replied SUPERMUM, grabbing all three. "The MOP OF MAYHEM! The AVENGING BUCKET OF DOOM! And, of course, the BOG BRUSH OF COSMIC CALAMITY!"

"Do they really work?" asked Galactic Girl.

"Well," began **SUPERMUM,** "all we have to do is believe!"

"I bagsie the **AVENGING BUCKET OF DOOM!**" demanded **ULTRABOY.**

"I wanted the **AVENGING BUCKET OF DOOM!** That's the best one!" moaned Galactic Girl.

"You can have the **MOP OF MAYHEM!**" said **SUPERMUM.**

"The **MOP OF MAYHEM** is lame!"

"No, it's not! It's the best one!"

"Ooh!" interrupted **ULTRABOY.** "I wanna swap the **AVENGING BUCKET OF DOOM** for the **MOP OF MAYHEM!**"

"Well, you can't!" snapped Galactic Girl.

"NOT FAIR!"

"*Come on, you two! No squabbling. We have a billion killer toilets to defeat!*"

Just then their own battered old bog began to gurgle.

GURGLE!

In no time, it had torn itself off the bathroom floor and was heading straight for them, snapping its seat as if it were jaws.

SNAP! SNAP! SNAP!

"*To the roof!*" ordered **SUPERMUM.**

"Why?" asked Galactic Girl.

"*I bet bogs can't **climb** up stairs!*"

BINGO! **SUPERMUM** was right. The three raced to the roof of their tower block, where they could see all over

London. Down below, bogs were still wreaking **havoc**, chasing people down the streets and gobbling them up in seconds.

"What do we have to do, Mum – I mean **SUPERMUM?**" asked Galactic Girl.

"We put our three weapons together, and we believe!"

"We believe what, exactly?"

"We believe that together they will create a bolt of super-lightning that will destroy these killer toilets once and for all."

"Well," began Galactic Girl, "it's worth a shot."

"It's the only hope we've got of saving the Earth," remarked ULTRABOY.

"Poor Earth," muttered Galactic Girl.

"ULTRABOY, Galactic Girl, **place the AVENGING BUCKET OF DOOM and the MOP OF MAYHEM next to my BOG BRUSH OF COSMIC CALAMITY."**

The two mini-superheroes did as they were asked.

CLUNK! went the three weapons together. But nothing happened.

"It's not working!" exclaimed the girl. "This is stupid. And I'm not GALACTIC GIRL! I am just plain old Punk."

"Let's all close our eyes," announced **SUPERMUM**, and they did so. **"BELIEVE!"**

Suddenly the three weapons began to rattle and hum, before...

Together they created a bolt of **super-lightning** that flew off the roof of the tower block and zapped in a billion different directions.

Exploding them into zillions of tiny pieces.

"WE'VE DONE IT!" shouted **ULTRABOY**, opening his eyes.

"I can't believe it. But I do believe it. We really have," said Galactic Girl, looking out across London to see the millions of smouldering bogs.

"Well done, my superhero chums!" said *SUPERMUM*. "So, how does it feel being Galactic Girl?"

Punk thought for a moment. "Pretty cool, actually."

"Then we three will **save** the Earth **once more!**" announced **SUPERMUM.** "It's all in a day's work for the three most super-duper-wuper superheroes of them all! **SUPERMUM!**"

"**ULTRABOY!**" exclaimed Spike.

"And **GALACTIC GIRL!**" Punk added proudly.

SUPERMUM smiled to herself.

She may be embarrassing, but at least they'd

saved the world!

THE
END